To To

THE PILOT

Enjoy the reading

by
Victoria Winters

Victoria 27.01.2014

Copyright © 2013 Victoria Winters

All rights reserved.

ISBN: 1-4905-6168-4
ISBN 13: 978-1-4905-6168-4
Library of Congress Control Number: 2013912307
CreateSpace Independent Publishing Platform,
North Charleston, South Carolina

To Deni
The person who never judged a book by its cover and left a pink footprint in the hearts of many people.

ACKNOWLEDGMENTS

First of all, I would like to thank my parents, Kris and Violeta, for their support. They have always believed in me and helped me when I needed them. Many thanks to my English teacher, Mrs Chonkova; if it weren't for her, I wouldn't have been able to publish this book. There were many people involved in this process, including Kristian Katsarov, who helped me with my personal website, and Nushka (one of my best friends), who gave me advice throughout and created many beautiful paintings which can be seen on my website. James and Octavio, thank you for helping me with the first chapters of this book; I really apreciate it. I have to thank Micha Nicheva for designing such a beautiful cover. She is very talented. And let's not forget my beautiful model—Milena and the handsome guy on the back cover - Martin. To all my friends who supported me and were always there for me: Ivan Boyadziev, Ivan Ilichov, Epitropov, Vasko, Kristina, Slenky, Nadia, Veronika Denizova, Stoyan, Wayne, Yoli, Adi, Radoslava, Mari Ya, and Karolina—I love you guys!

"What if I'm your only chance of happiness? You haven't realised it yet, but you will one day."

PROLOGUE

People say that before you die, you see your life as if it were a movie. All the things you've done, all the places you've ever visited, all the people you know. But how can you think about the past when you know that there will be no future for you? You won't be able to see your loved ones ever again. You won't be able to feel their touch, to smell their scent. You won't be able to look in your mother's eyes or kiss your lover.

For me, death was a synonym for fear, pain, sorrow, but that all changed at the moment I realised that I was falling, I was losing control, and I couldn't do anything about it. I knew that I didn't have much time left on this planet, in this life, but I wasn't afraid. I was calm. I overcame my fear, because I was sure that, somewhere, there was something beautiful, something new and exciting. Something I'd never felt before in my life. I was going to have a new beginning, a clean start, without pain or hatred. My mistakes were about to be forgotten, and all the bad things I'd ever done would become history.

I saw the green mountains of Scotland, where my grandparents used to take me for walks and picnics. I smelled the scent of fresh-cut grass in our back garden, where I used to play. I remembered the beauty of Windsor Castle, near where I grew up, and where my friends and I used to pretend that we were guards of Her Majesty. I heard the voice of the sea and felt the wet sand under my feet, and I remembered the place where I first met her. I enjoyed the silence of the parks in London, where I used to hide from all the noise and the people who lived there. I saw the giant tree we used to have picnics beneath, and I cried.

I wasn't thinking about the pain my death would cause everybody. For the first time in my life, I wasn't thinking about me. I was thinking about her. I will never forget her green eyes, shining like emeralds, full of life. She had the most beautiful smile in the world. Her lips were the colour of a pink Princess Diana rose. I really loved her, and I always will. She was the reason I was here. She was the one who showed me the right way, the one who saved me. She was always there for me. I will remember the jasmine in her curly brown hair, that I could smell when she was embracing me, when she was wiping away my tears.

The thought of her made me cry once again, and I was unable to stop my tears from falling. At the very end of my life, I could only think about her.

I no longer heard the lieutenant on the radio. I didn't hear anything, not even the sound of my plane falling. It was all quiet. The only thing I heard was her voice, her gentle voice, saying, "I love you, Ben! I will always love you!"

I didn't have air, and it was so hard to breathe. But I didn't feel pain, not even in my shoulder, which had been hit by a bullet ten minutes ago. Time was passing very slowly, just like a slow-motion scene from a movie. I thought that everything would end very fast, in just a second, but it didn't. I wasn't going to feel any pain when the plane crashed.

I closed my eyes. It was almost time for me to say good-bye to this world and to pray that God would forgive me for all my mistakes.

In my last moments, I started seeing my life: my mistakes, my offences, my criminal record. At the end, I saw her. She was smiling at me. I saw her white teeth, shining like pearls. The girl I loved was waiting for me to come to her, to hug her, to kiss her again. She was the last thing I saw before the plane crashed.

CHAPTER 1

I remember the first time I saw an aeroplane. I was five, and it was the happiest moment of my life to that point. My father was a pilot and my hero. He was part of the Royal Air Force, and I was very proud of him. Unfortunately, he was always away, and I saw him only two or three times a year, if I was lucky. It's not easy when you are an air commodore, after all. He was always putting his missions first, but I knew that he loved me very much, and he was going to do everything he could for Mum and me.

My mother was working in a hospital as a nurse when she met him. He fell while playing football with his boys and twisted his ankle. Silly, isn't it? A strong man like him, a soldier and all, to twist his ankle whilst playing football. He joked with her in front of the doctor the whole time, and at the end he asked for her phone number, but she didn't give it to him. He kept coming day after day, asking for her number, until she finally agreed to go out with him. Every time she looked back, she said that he was the best thing in her life, because he was the reason she had me. She was never sorry for marrying him, even though she knew that he wouldn't be around all the time.

But my father was a great dad. He took me fishing whenever he was home. He always came back with lots of gifts for me and my mum. They couldn't compensate for his absence, but I was always happy to receive a new toy, gun, or soldier figure. I still remember his voice saying, "Hello again, little soldier!" every time he returned. Dad used to play with me and my figures, pretending that we were on the battlefield, preparing to meet our enemies. We made so much noise that my mum would come in and say, "OK, you two, it's time to finish this battle. Dinner is ready!" Then I'd jump on his shoulders, and he would take me to the table.

When I was five years old, he took me to the Royal Air Force Museum in London to see a real battle aeroplane. He told me many stories about his fellow soldiers, who helped him in difficult situations and saved his life. He told me stories about the air force, the planes, and all the places he'd been to. Sometimes I saw tears in his eyes—when he told me how some of his friends had died and hadn't managed to get back to their families. I think that, in a way, Dad felt guilty about this, but he wasn't able to predict what would happen in a battle. He was proud of what he did. My father was sure that one day I would do exactly the same. I would join the air force and become a pilot, just like him. Maybe this was one of the reasons he talked about aeroplanes so much. The other was that he loved them. Except for spending time with my mum and me, for him there was nothing better than flying a powerful machine like a SEPECAT Jaguar, which can fly up to 1,056 miles per hour.

We woke up early that day, around six o'clock in the morning. Mum was still sleeping, but my dad was a trained soldier, and he never woke up later than six. Sometimes he had trouble sleeping. I still remember his screams late at night, and how Mum comforted him after every nightmare he had. It must have been very tough for him to be away from his family and watch his friends die in the field. I didn't realise that until I started following in his footsteps.

My father opened the door of my room very carefully. He didn't want to scare me. He entered the room and whispered, "Ben, it's time to wake up, little soldier. We are going to the RAF Museum today." He lifted my blanket, but he didn't find me there. "Ben? Where are you?"

Suddenly, I came from behind him, roaring, and jumped on his back. "Do you give up?" I said.

"Yes, yes, you defeated me," he replied, after I pushed him onto the floor.

I heard my mum coming from the other room. "What are you two doing? What's all that noise?"

Dad lifted me onto his shoulders. I felt like a giant at that moment. "Nothing, love, we were just playing. Little soldier here ambushed me and jumped on my shoulders."

"Ben, how many times have I told you not to attack your father?"

"It's OK, Caroline. Don't worry. If he wants to be a real soldier one day, he has to learn how to defend himself."

"We'll see about that, Patrick. So, since everybody's up, who's cooking breakfast?"

"That would be me, I guess."

"Good answer." They both laughed, and he kissed her on the cheek. Mum reminded me that I had to wash my teeth and my face before breakfast. Then she went back to their bedroom to get dressed.

After we'd all eaten Dad's delicious English breakfast, Mum helped me to get dressed. She filled my bag with juice, apples, a chocolate bar, and my little soldiers and my aeroplanes. We were ready to leave now.

Mum drove us to the station. She decided to do some shopping, because she had the whole day all to herself. After giving birth to me, she hadn't gone back to work. She had to take care of me all the time while Dad wasn't around, and she was a great mother.

She left us near the castle, and we walked to the station. I've always admired the castle—so beautiful and so mysterious. My father hated driving in London. He always said that it was suicide. You could never find a parking space, and you were always stuck in traffic. That's why we were travelling by train.

"Are you excited that you are going to see your first aeroplane?"

"I can't wait. Daddy, are they going to let me inside one of them?"

"I doubt that, champ. But I can take you with me to the hangar where we keep our planes and show you mine."

"Wow! And are we going to fly it?"

"I'm afraid not. But one day, you will have your own, better and faster than mine."

"Promise?"

"I promise."

After we got off the train, we took the Northern line to Colindale and walked for about ten minutes to the museum. The weather was warm and sunny, so Dad decided that we could have a picnic in the park after we finished the tour of the museum.

The entrance of the museum looked like an old military base. I was so excited that I couldn't stop jumping up and down, as I held my father's hand. Once we entered, I didn't know which way to look first. There were so many things that I wanted to see. I ran from one display to another. Since I wasn't able to read, I dragged Dad to every map, every label, and every picture so he could read them to me and give me more details about all the exhibits. But my favourite of all the collections was the Bomber Hall Aircraft Collection. Some of the aircraft there were really funny. For example the K2's nose looked like a fugu fish that was trying to attack. It was designed to be a strategic nuclear bomber, after all. I couldn't imagine how anyone could fly that thing, or how it was able to make a whole town vanish just by dropping a single bomb.

"Daddy, what's that funny thing over there? It looks like a double bed."

"It's an FE2b from the First World War. Believe it or not, son, this thing can reach a speed of ninety-two miles per hour. It can..."

"And what's that, Daddy?"

"That's a..."

"Daddy, Daddy, look! This one looks like a swordfish!"

"It's a Hawker Siddeley Buccaneer and...Ben, Ben, stop running around, or they will kick us out!"

"But there are so many. I want to see all of them!"

"We have plenty of time, champ. Don't worry."

"We won't have time to go to the other halls!"

"We will. Now have a look at this one. It's my favourite. It's a V Bomber. Do you know why it's called a V Bomber?

"No. Why?"

"Because there were three types of bombers, which were developed between 1950 and 1960. Their names were Vickers Valiant, Avro Vulcan, and Handley Page Victor. They were also known as the V Class."

I stood there looking at the Avro Vulcan, thinking how beautiful it was, with all its military colours and insignia of the Royal Air Force on it, and I realised that I wanted to be a pilot, just like my dad. I was meant to be one. It was in my blood.

We visited the Historic Hangars, where I saw the Supermarine Stranraer and the Taylorcraft Auster I, with wings that looked like a dachshund's ears. There were a few other hangars, full of aeroplanes, pictures, and uniforms. One part of the Bomber Hall was all about Princess Mary's Royal Air Force Nursing Services. As I went in, I thought of my mum. I started imagining how my parents had met, what their first date was like, and how much they loved each other. I was five, and even I was able to see the tenderness in their eyes.

On our way out of the museum, we passed by the gift shop. I wanted to buy something there to remember this day. I couldn't make up my mind from among all the pictures of aeroplanes, little soldier toys, and key rings. While I was wandering around the shop, from shelf to shelf, my father came to me with a little replica of an Avro Vulcan, almost identical to the one we'd seen inside the Bomber Hall. The perfect choice.

"Daddy, where are we going now?"

"To Brent Reservoir."

"What is that?"

"It looks like a lake with many trees around it. We can sit there and have lunch, and you can feed the ducks."

"Why can't we go to McDonald's?"

"Because I want you to enjoy the nice weather outside."

"All right. But I want you to take me to McDonald's tomorrow."

"OK, I promise. Let's get on the bus now."

It took us around twenty minutes to get there, but it was worth it. There were so many trees. The grass looked fresh, and I could smell it. I couldn't believe that you could have such a beautiful place in a huge city like London. I was used to the parks in Windsor, the big green fields, and the river, but this was the first time I'd seen such a big lake. Ducks were swimming in it, quacking and making noise. Birds flew overhead, and it was very quiet, as if we were outside the city. A few boats passed by the place where we were sitting, and I waved at them.

"I want to show you something. Come. Take a stone, and get ready to throw it in the water."

"Like this?"

"No, look at me. See how I'm holding the stone? Oh, you've taken the wrong one. It has to be flat."

"There's one over there."

"Right! Now get ready. Slowly throw it in the water, like this."

"Wow! Let me try, Daddy."

"Wait, let me show you."

He took my hand, moved my body closer to the water, and asked me to bend down a little. Then he showed me how to move my hand and throw the stone in the water so it would jump like a frog. It didn't work the first five times, but the sixth was a success. The stone jumped only twice, but I was so excited that I had made progress, I couldn't stop trying.

"Look, Daddy, I did it!"

"You are my champion! Now, come here and eat yours sandwich."

"Hey, what is that? I've never seen one before."

"Shhh! It's a pheasant. Quiet. They get scared very easily.

"It's so beautiful! Wow, look at its feathers!"

"Are you glad that we didn't go to McDonald's now?"

"I am."

"Let's play with your little soldiers."

After an hour of walking around the lake and enjoying the view, Dad decided that it was time for us to go back to Windsor. I was so tired that I slept all the way home. Mom was waiting for us at the train station, and the three of us went for dinner at Pizza Express, one of my favourite places after McDonald's. She'd been so busy shopping all day with her friends that she hadn't had time to prepare dinner. But it was the best ending to the last day I was to spend with my father. He was leaving the next day. He had to go back to his base. I was never going to forget this day. It was one of happiest of my life, not counting the day I met her.

CHAPTER 2

It was late in the evening. I was putting on my pyjamas, getting ready to go to bed, when the phone rang. I ran downstairs, thinking that it must be Daddy calling. He had been away for more than a year. He hadn't even come back for Christmas, but he managed to send us a postcard. He called only once a month, but he sent us letters regularly. I knew that Dad was supposed to come home in two weeks, and I was really looking forward to seeing him again, because I had missed him more than ever. I was starting school that autumn, and I wanted to talk to him about it.

"Hello?" Mum answered the phone.

"Is this Mrs Johnson?"

"Yes. Who is it?"

"Mrs Johnson, my name is General Steven Watson. I'm one of your husband's colleagues. I think that you might want to sit down. I'm afraid I've got some bad news."

I ran into the living room when I saw how my mum slid down the sofa and covered her face with her hands, crying. I saw the tears coming out of her hazel eyes and falling down her pale cheeks.

"Who was it, Mummy? Was it Daddy?" I tugged at her sleeve. "Why didn't you call me? I wanted to talk to him. Mummy, why are you crying?" She wiped her face again and smiled at me. I could see the pain in her eyes, which had turned red from the tears.

"Ben, I want you to sit down, honey."

"What's wrong, Mummy?"

"I want you to be strong and remember how much I love you, OK?"

"Is it about Daddy? He's not coming back in two weeks, is he? He's been held there, like always."

"I think that it's more serious this time, love."

I knew what she was going to say. She wiped her face with a tissue, for the third time, and hugged me. I felt my mum's heartbeat; it was jumping like mad. I had never seen her like this before. I was able to sense her pain, even though she tried to hide it from me.

"Mummy, is he dead?"

"Ben, I don't know how to say this. One of your daddy's colleagues just called to tell me that your father got shot by a Bosnian soldier. His friends did everything possible to save him, but they couldn't. He'd lost too much blood, honey." She stopped for a moment to take a breath. Tears were trying to come out of her eyes, but she was strong enough to stop them from falling.

"He was trying to protect a boy by pushing him out of the line of fire, and a bullet hit him in the chest. I'm so sorry, baby. Remember that your father was a hero, and he loved you more than anything."

"Mummy, is Daddy an angel now?"

"Yes, sweetie, he is. He can fly in the sky as much as he wants now."

"What are we going to do now, Mummy?"

"I don't know, baby. I don't know…"

My mother hugged me, and I felt her warm body. She couldn't hold her tears back anymore, and they started falling from her eyes like raindrops. My father and I were everything she had in this world. She'd lost her parents a few years before. And now Dad was gone. I couldn't imagine how she felt at that moment, not until I lost the one I loved.

The government paid all the expenses for the transport of my father's body and his funeral. It arrived in a coffin four days after the phone call. Those four days were extremely tough for my mother. She had to call all of his friends and relatives, including his parents. It isn't easy to deal with the funeral preparations for the only person you've ever loved. She ordered the flowers, red and orange gerberas, which were his favourites. The wreath was made of white callas, like the flowers he'd given her on their first date. She ordered food—canapés and drinks—for the reception at our house.

On the day of the funeral, I had to wake up early. My mother gave me a shower and told me that I had to wear a suit. Grandma and Grandpa had arrived from Wales the night before. They were both devastated. Grandma couldn't stop crying. My mother was trying to stay calm and strong, but I knew that she was heartbroken. I heard her crying all night on the day she received the news and every single night after that. I didn't know what to do to soothe her. I was just a six-year-old kid who had lost his father.

I heard a few birds singing in the backyard. They were in the apple tree, probably waiting for someone to feed them. My father used to do that when he was home. They didn't realise that he was not coming back. For a moment I envied them, because they looked so calm. They didn't feel pain. The only thing they cared about was their breakfast. Their life was so easy, just like mine had been a few days before. But everything had changed in just one night. I was frightened, because I didn't know what was coming or what we were going to do. The loss of my father forced me to grow up quickly. From now on I was going to be the head of our family, so I had to be strong for both my mother and me. I was just a little kid, but my dad had shown me how to be responsible, how to take care of my mother. I guess that he'd been preparing me for this day, because he knew that sooner or later, he was going to lose his life.

My mother called me to have breakfast with my grandmother and grandfather, and I ran back to the kitchen. I wasn't hungry at all, but I had to eat something, because I didn't want to upset them.

I took my favourite Spiderman plate that was already piled with scrambled eggs, two sausages, and a few hash browns. I was surprised that Mum had prepared an English breakfast for all of us, but she needed to do something to keep herself occupied. She didn't like having an English breakfast every morning. She cooked it only once every two or three months, usually when she was upset, because she was crazy about healthy eating. To her, having this cholesterol bomb for breakfast was suicide. Besides, it took a lot of time to prepare.

The whole house was full of flowers; our living room looked like a huge buffet in a Chinese restaurant where you pay twelve quid and can eat as much as you want. The weather outside was nice and sunny, so my grandfather decided to put several tables in the backyard, and Grandma put the rest of the food on them.

First we had to go to the cemetery, where my father's colleagues paid him their last respects and escorted him to his resting place. Everybody was dressed in black, except the twelve soldiers. I will never forget how my mother was dressed. She wore a skirt, a jacket, and an enormous hat, all black. She wore sunglasses to hide her red eyes and the shadows below them. All the guests walked with their heads down. It was so difficult to accept that this man, in perfect health and only forty years old, had lost his life.

The funeral was very solemn. The soldiers were dressed in uniform. Six of the twelve marched in front of the coffin, holding rifles. The rest carried the coffin, and the family walked behind it. When we reached the graveside, everybody gathered around. The priest gave a speech. I didn't pay attention to what he was saying, because I didn't care. I guess that he mentioned something about Dad's fights, how he had saved someone else's life but lost his own, that he was a good father and husband, and how sad it was that he was gone. I didn't want to listen to this. I only wanted my father back.

After the speech was over, my father's coffin was lowered into the grave. General Mason gave orders to the soldiers to shoot in the air. I heard four shots. Then all of the soldiers, including the general, saluted. All of them turned and left the cemetery.

Most of Dad's colleagues and friends came to our house after the funeral. They were all sympathetic. They told my mother Dad was a great man and they would miss him. They were aware that the words coming out of their mouths didn't mean anything to her, but they couldn't change what had happened to her only love. Even though the sentences were clichés, they had nothing else to offer.

While everybody was eating and talking, a woman with blonde hair approached my mother. I had never seen her before, and by the look on my mother's face, she hadn't either. She was very short, but compared to my mother, who was almost six feet tall, everybody looked short.

"Mrs Johnson, I would like to thank you. I know that this is not the right moment, but I would like to thank you for having such a brave husband."

"Thank you."

"If it wasn't for your husband, my son would be dead."

My mother's face changed when she heard this. Her sunglasses and black hat were off now. Everybody could see her pain, but no one was able to feel it. She looked into this woman's eyes and saw regret and relief at the same time. Mum realised who the woman was, and when she saw the brown-haired young man next to her, her suspicion was confirmed. He was around twenty-five years old, tall, and dressed in a uniform. I realised now that he was one of the soldiers who had marched in front of the coffin.

"This is my son, Michael."

"Nice to meet you, ma'am. I am so sorry about your husband. He was a great man."

"Thank you, Michael. So you are the boy he saved."

"Yes, ma'am."

I wasn't sure, but I thought that I saw my mother smiling, as though she was feeling relief. Now that she'd met the young man whom my father had saved, she knew that he hadn't lost his life because he wasn't careful. He had acted as he did because he couldn't imagine how this poor woman would live without her only son. All the anger she had been keeping in her heart was gone. She was a mother as well, and she couldn't imagine what would happen to her life if I was killed.

When everybody had left, my grandparents and my mother cleaned the whole house. Grandma washed the dishes. Grandpa put all the extra tables in his van, so he could return them to the rental company. I sat on my bed, looking at the last aeroplane my father had given me. When my mother entered the room, she saw me crying.

"Oh, baby, I miss him, too."

"I know, Mummy, but I can't stop it."

"I know, sweetie. Just let it go. The pain will go away with time."

"Do you promise?"

"Yes. Now go to bed. It's late."

"I love you, Mummy!"

"I love you, too, honey. Good night and sweet dreams."

CHAPTER 3

After my father's funeral, my mother had to talk to an accountant to find out how much money we had and how to manage the mortgage. She didn't know what to do, because Dad was the one who took care of all the payments and bank accounts. He was the one who worked and looked after the family, but now he was gone. She had to find a job and go on with her life.

But it wasn't easy. My mother found a job as a nurse at the local hospital. She had to work long shifts. Sometimes she had to be there all day. There were more expenses than she had expected. I had just started going to school. She had to have a nanny stay with me for the whole night, because she couldn't leave me alone, and even though her salary was quite high, she couldn't manage to cover all the bills. Grandma visited from time to time, for a week or two, but it wasn't enough.

We lived in our Windsor house for two more years, and then my mother decided to sell it. She found a job at North Middlesex Hospital in London, and because she couldn't afford to travel every day, we moved to London. I was just getting used to the primary school I was attending when she moved me to the Lancasterian Primary School. I didn't want to leave Windsor, where my best friends were. I didn't want to move to another house, because this was my father's house. He chose it; he bought it. I had grown up in this house. I couldn't just leave it like this for someone else, someone I didn't know. I was angry at my mother. I was only eight years old, too young to realise that we didn't have any choice.

On my first day at the new school, my mother received a call from the head teacher. She was at work, but since my school was only fifteen minutes away from the hospital, she asked to take her break earlier. I didn't think about what my actions could cause back then. I didn't realise how difficult it must have been for my mother to deal with all the stress I was causing her.

"Mrs Johnson, thanks for coming. I am Catherine Tyler, the head teacher."

"I apologise for being late. I was at work, and I was very busy."

"It's OK, Mrs Johnson. I called you because it seems that Ben doesn't like his new school."

"What do you mean?"

"Well, he's not talking to anyone. He's staying away from his schoolmates. But that is not what bothers me."

"What is it?"

"Today one of the kids tried to talk to Ben. David approached him and asked him if he wanted to play, but Ben didn't reply. He just stood there, staring at the grass. David asked him again. Ben still didn't answer. One of his classmates heard David call Ben weird, and your son punched David. David punched him back."

"Oh my God, is he OK?"

"He's with the school nurse. He'll be OK. But I have to tell you, Mrs Johnson, that I am very worried about your son. It's not a good sign when an eight-year-old boy doesn't communicate with his peers and fights with them for no reason."

"I understand, Mrs Tyler, but you have to understand that it is really tough for him at the moment. He had to leave the house he'd lived in all his life. He had say good-bye to all his friends there, and he doesn't know anyone here. He is very angry with me, because he thinks that this is all my fault. I am doing twelve-hour shifts, and I don't have time for him. He is just a lonely child."

"I know this, Mrs Johnson, but you have to do something about it, because he might get even more violent in time."

"I will take care of it."

And she tried, but with no success. She asked for shorter shifts at the hospital, morning shifts, so she could spend more time with me. But, as she said, I was just a kid. I couldn't understand how much she loved me, and I didn't care about all the things she did for me. I didn't appreciate that she came to pick me up from school every day or that she helped me with my homework and took me for playdays in the park. And I didn't stop fighting with my classmates. I bullied a different kid every week, and as a result, I changed schools five times in three years.

By the age of fourteen, I had become uncontrollable. I fought with my mum every evening about coming home late, my school grades, bringing friends home while she was at work, making the whole flat one big mess. I had changed completely. I had no goals, no regrets about what I was doing, no respect for my mother, and apparently no future. I dressed like a thug. My blue eyes were hidden behind sunglasses, my black hair was covered with a hat, and my trousers were halfway down my backside. I wore T-shirts, or a hoodie to cover my milky-white hands when it was cold.

My mother pushed me to study hard, go to college, and get a university degree. She was still hoping that I would change my attitude, realise how important it was to have good marks at school, and think about the future. But I spent every day playing video games, sleeping till late, skipping classes, and not caring about anyone except myself.

When I was sixteen, I went to a party at the house of some friends. Kevin and his twin brother, Nigel, brought some skunk from somewhere, and we all got high. This was the first time I had used drugs, and I loved it. We all got drunk. I went home covered with puke and staggering. My mother was waiting for me in the living room. I didn't know what time it was, but it must have been very late. She looked at me as though I had just committed a crime, and she was the judge.

"Where have you been?"

"None of your business."

"It is, because you are my son, and I am responsible for you. Do you know what time it is?"

"I don't care."

"Ben, don't talk to me like that! I am your mother. I don't deserve this!"

"Just go away and leave me alone, woman."

"Are you drunk? Your eyes are red."

"Don't touch me!"

I caught my mother's hand as she tried to touch my face. I didn't know what I was doing. I was confused, drunk, and on drugs. She tried to free her hand, but she couldn't because I was holding her very tight. I could see the pain I was causing her, but I didn't want to let her go. I was so angry, so confused. She tried to slap me with her left hand, but I caught it. I pushed her down on the floor and hissed at her to leave me alone. Her curly black hair was splayed out on the carpet, and tears fell from her hazel eyes. I ran to my room and locked the door, but I could still hear her crying. The only problem was that I didn't care.

CHAPTER 4

I never apologised for what I'd done to my mother that night, and even worse, I fought with her almost every day. She screamed at me; I shouted at her. We didn't get along, and it was very difficult for us to live together. I now realise what she was trying to do, how she was trying to help and guide me, and how much she loved me. But back in those days, I hated her for not understanding me, not supporting me. When I think about what I was doing when I was sixteen, I know she had every right to be angry at me, to be worried about what could happen to me.

I got drunk all the time, and I smoked skunk like a chimney. I brought different girls home almost every night. I didn't even know their names. I would meet a girl at a party at Nigel and Kevin's house, we would snog there for a while, and then I would take her to my room. I remembered their names at the beginning—Katie, Lexie, Natasha, Maria, but after Jane, I didn't even make an effort to memorize their faces or their names. They were all the same—trashy women who were looking for one-night stands. There was no point in remembering anything about them, because I wasn't looking for a serious relationship or love. I didn't need it, until I met her. She showed me what real love means, what it is to love someone and to be loved. If it hadn't been for her, I would've wandered around the world without any purpose at all for the rest of my life. She managed to save me, and I would blame myself my whole life for not saving her.

My mother was worried for me. She didn't want me to catch some venereal disease or become a player who didn't respect women, who used them and threw them away like used tissues. She was tired of me coming back late and making noise. I can't imagine how difficult it must have been for her. She worked night shifts at the hospital, and the only thing she wanted when she came home was to go to sleep. But her ungrateful son couldn't understand that.

"Who was the girl leaving your room early this morning?"

"Sarah...Tara...I don't remember. Does it matter?"

"Of course it does. She is the fifth girl you've brought home this week."

"What do you care?"

"I'm worried about you. I'm your mother, after all."

"What are you doing in my room?"

"You have exams in two weeks. Why aren't you studying?"

"Leave me alone! I want to sleep."

"I was planning to go to sleep an hour ago, but then you started making noise."

I pushed my mother out of my room, closed the door after her, and locked it. She was too tired, weak, and tired to try to oppose me. I heard her go back to her room and close the door. Even though she was extremely tired, I knew that she wouldn't get any sleep at all.

I never sat on my butt to study hard for exams, as I should have. But somehow I managed to pass my GCSE exams and get into college. Since I didn't have many options, I took a course on building construction at a local college. That's where my friends Kevin and Nigel had signed up. They were my best mates. We partied all night, hitting on girls, smoking, and riding bikes together. All of us shared the feeling that we didn't want to go to college, but we had no choice. Our parents said that we had to either study or find jobs. Since we were lazy and were used to taking money from our parents, we chose college.

At the beginning of the semester, it was amazingly easy. I didn't even attend lectures or practice. I didn't think that my mother would find out, but when the results from the first semester came, she wasn't pleased at all. I'd failed four out of six exams and had to resit two of my assignments. My mother couldn't bear this situation anymore. She couldn't see a way to change me. She realised that I was going down a road from which there was no way back.

One night, I came home early. I was alone, and I wanted only to go to bed and rest. But when I entered the dining room, I saw my mother having dinner with a man I didn't know. She seemed confused when she saw me. I guess that she wasn't expecting me to be home so early.

"Ben, do you want to have dinner with us?"

"I'm not hungry. Who's this guy?"

"This is Stephen. We work together."

"Is that what you call it these days—working together?"

"Ben, please be polite. We have a guest."

"He's your guest, not mine. I didn't invite him here to have fun. I'm going to my room. I hope that you won't be making a lot of noise. I want to sleep."

My mother didn't try to stop me, because she knew what would happen. I wasn't in the mood to meet this guy. I didn't want to talk to him. When he stood up and tried to shake my hand, I pulled my hand back and ran from the room.

I heard them when they left the flat after dinner. I didn't even want to know where they were going. When did this happen? When did she forget about my father? How could I have been so blind? I was so angry with my mother for not telling me about this. But how could she? When I did spend time with her, we fought. I was nice to her only when I wanted to get something from her—or on her birthday, if I hadn't forgotten about it. I wondered how many years she'd spent alone all day, waiting for me to change, to give her at least one compliment, to be nice to her for more than ten minutes.

My mother was waiting for me in the dining room the next morning. She had prepared an English breakfast. She was wearing her uniform, because she had to go to work. I sat at the table without saying anything to her, not even good morning, and I started eating.

"Good morning!" she said.

"It's good for some people, for others not so much."

"Look, Ben, I didn't want you to find out about Stephen and me this way."

"Then why did you bring him to our house? How long has this been going on?"

"A few months. In case you're wondering, he is the first man I've seen since your father passed away."

"Why would I care? It's your life, not mine. You didn't respect my wish to stay and live in Windsor; why would you respect my father's memory?"

"I didn't want to move here either. You know why we did. We had no choice."

"I don't care! Do whatever you want to do. You don't care about my opinion, anyway."

"Ben, listen to me. You have to grow up. You are not a child anymore. Please, stop being angry with me. I don't deserve it!"

"Says who?"

"I'm tired of this."

"Yeah? Well, I'm tired of you, as well. I'm going back to my room. And don't bother looking for me or calling me for the next few days. I'm staying at Nigel's."

She took her bag and left for work. I finished my breakfast and put some clothes in a bag. I'd lied to her. I wasn't going to Nigel's house. We were going to Brighton for the weekend with a guy named Josh. He was Kevin's friend, and he was five years older than us. I had no idea what we were going to do, but I was always ready for an adventure. Kevin said that these two days were going to change my life forever, and he was right.

CHAPTER 5

Josh was one of those guys who cares only about himself. He was a tricky one. You never knew what he was thinking or what he was planning to do next. He smiled at you and at the same time was making plans behind your back, plans that could ruin your life. He always knew how to get what he wanted. His brown eyes inspired respect and fear, but never hope or love. He knew how to earn money without lifting a finger. He was my idol. I would have turned into him and wandered around all alone without any purpose in life, living a life full of lies, if she hadn't come into my life and changed it.

"Are you ready for the party tonight, boys?"

"What do you think?" said Nigel, smiling at him.

"You have to do something for me tonight. Nothing comes for free, guys, especially with me."

"Whatever you say, bro."

"I want you to sell some grass. You'll get some money for the favour you're doing me, of course."

"Can we keep some for ourselves?"

"Ben, mate, you're my buddies. Sure you can, as long as you pay for it."

The three of us got very excited, because we were going to earn some money and keep something for ourselves. I can't believe how stupid I was to have friends like Josh, Nigel, and Kevin. They were dragging me down. I was going to ruin my future by selling skunk, coke, and God knows what else. But I was too young to realise it.

The party was at a house near the beach. Josh said that it belonged to some chick whose parents were out of the country at the moment. By the look of the house, I could see that these people had a lot of money. I could tell that there were at least five bedrooms in the house without even going inside. The front garden was well maintained. There was a path leading to the front door and another one leading to the three garages under the house.

Josh pressed a button on the intercom and told somebody that we were waiting outside. After two minutes, a chocolate girl with green eyes—probably contact lenses—and curly hair came out of the front door and opened the gates for us. She threw herself on Josh and started kissing him. Josh chose his girlfriends very carefully, and he knew how to make them fall in love with him. This chick was amazingly hot. She looked as though she was twenty-one years old, and she had a well-fit body with big boobs. Besides, her parents were so rich they could afford anything to satisfy all her wishes, which made her even more attractive to a guy like Josh, who used others to get what he wanted. He wasn't stupid at all. This girl looked as if she was really into him, but I was 100 per cent sure that he was using her.

"You're late."

"I had to pick up the guys from the station, love, and instruct them."

"What do you have for me?"

"Only the best for my beautiful queen." He gave her a small package with white powder inside it—probably coke. She put it in the back pocket of her Armani jeans and kissed him again.

"These guys are Ben, Nigel, and Kevin. They came from London for the weekend."

"I'm Maggie. Nice to meet you, boys. What are you waiting for? Come on in and have fun."

The living room was larger than my flat and full of drunken people. They all had glasses or fags in their hands. The music was loud, and there was a real DJ at the end of the room. He was mixing hip-hop and house music. A strange combination, but it seemed that everybody loved it. Some chicks were dancing on the table half naked, and others were snogging with guys on the sofas. I was sure that at least one of the five bedrooms in the house was occupied. It doesn't matter how much money you have; when you go to a party, you always end up drunk, sleeping on the floor half naked, or in bed with someone you've never seen before. I walked around the room and talked to a few people. In an hour, I'd managed to sell all the packages Josh gave me. A few girls tried their luck with me, but I wasn't in the mood. I'd come here to have fun, and I didn't need someone to chase after me all night.

I decided to go out and light a fag. Even though the music inside the house was very loud, when I stepped into the garden and shut the front door, I could hear only the waves of the sea. It was a little windy, but warm at the same time. I headed to one of the benches next to the fountain, and then I saw her. She was sitting on the wooden bench and looking at the stars. The moonlight lit up her brown hair.

"I didn't see you at the party."

"Because I wasn't there." She stood up and stepped back from the bench. I felt as if she was afraid of me.

"Hey, I'm not gonna eat you. Stay here for a while, and keep me company."

"Sorry, you're not my type."

"You don't even know me."

"You came to Maggie's party. Trust me. I know exactly what kind of person you are." She gave me a piercing look, and then I noticed her beautiful green eyes, glittering like emeralds in the moonlight.

"What are you doing here, then, since you didn't come for the party? Are you going to rob the house after everybody's drunk, and they don't know what they're doing?"

"If I was waiting for everybody to get drunk, I would've been gone by now with half of the jewellery. I'm waiting for Karisha. She's Maggie's younger sister."

A skinny girl, who looked like a shorter version of Maggie, came down the path. She was smiling at first, but when she saw me sitting on the bench next to the girl, she literally ran to where we were sitting. I guess that Karisha was worried that I might do something to her friend.

"Daniela, have you been waiting for a long time?"

"Nope, just ten minutes. Shall we go?"

"Sure. Let's go."

"It was nice talking to you," I said. She turned around, but she didn't say anything. I followed her with my eyes until she went through the front gate and closed it after her. This was the first time in my life that a girl did not want to talk to me, didn't want to stay with me, and instead went off with her friend. Girls were usually fighting for me, crying because of me. She didn't even tell me her name. I knew that this girl was going to change my life, because I couldn't stop thinking about her all night.

I woke up very early the next morning. I'd fallen asleep on one of the sofas in the living room, and when I opened my eyes, I saw many drunken people from last night lying on the carpet. I hadn't drunk at all that night, which was not typical for me. Nigel asked if I was sick. But I didn't want to get drunk, because I was afraid that I'd forget her face. I didn't know why I was still thinking about her—maybe because she was very beautiful, or maybe because she cut me off without even giving me a chance. I knew how to impress a girl, but this was different. She wasn't like any other girl I'd known.

Kevin came downstairs. I guess that he must have slept with some girl he'd met last night, and he was trying to sneak out without waking her up. He complained about having a horrible hangover, because he'd mixed vodka with skunk and a girl, and he didn't have any memory of the party. I asked him if he wanted to come with me to Starbucks to have a coffee and then breakfast at McDonald's. He welcomed the idea of a double cheeseburger with french fries and mozzarella dippers. Besides, he needed caffeine so badly that he would kill somebody for it. Unfortunately he wasn't good company, because he could barely talk. His eyes were as red as a traffic light.

But once we were out in the fresh air, he started talking about the party the night before, or at least about what he remembered from it, until we reached Starbucks. "Where were you last night? You disappeared."

"You just don't remember. I was around, man, talking to the girls."

I wasn't in the mood to tell him where I'd been or about Daniela. I knew that he would make fun of me. Kevin and Nigel were Josh's clones, but unlike him, they were both very stupid. The twins didn't have their own opinions. They listened to whatever Josh said to them. He was their god.

When we went into Starbucks, Kevin was just explaining to me that the girl he'd been with last night was incredibly beautiful and well fit. I wasn't listening to him at all. I was sick of his stories. Besides, he was always exaggerating. I did the same stuff he did—going to parties, having sex with different girls every time—but I didn't like talking about it. It was my business what I did and with whom. But at that moment I was thinking about only one girl: Daniela. I wouldn't have known her name if it wasn't for Karisha.

And there she was. She was waiting at the till to pay. A few meters away from her, Karisha was waving her hand to get Daniela's attention. I couldn't believe my eyes. I'd thought that I would never see her again.

"Good morning!" I said to her, but she looked at me as though I'd just slapped her in the face. She replied though. I guess the girl was too polite to pass by me without saying anything. Daniela took her hot chocolate from the counter and joined Karisha at her table.

"Man, she's not for you."

"What do you mean?"

"I saw the way you were looking at her. Forget it. She's not one of ours, she's a good girl, a smart girl. I bet she's a virgin."

"Shut up, Kevin!"

"Oh, you like her! Ben and Daniela sitting in a tree. K-i-s-s-i-n-g..."

"Kevin, if you don't shut your fucking mouth, I'll kick your black ass out of this coffee shop!"

"Hey, man, no need to be rude. I was only joking. So...do you like her?"

"I don't know her, you idiot. I've just met her. How come you know her name?"

"She's Maggie's sister's friend. They're studying together. She lives down the street, in a white house. But she's not for you, man. Karisha and Daniela live in a different world. Oh, man, if I could just get this girl for one night, I would enjoy it. Actually I wouldn't mind having the two sisters together. Give me five."

I hit Kevin's hand a little harder than he expected. I was sure that he felt pain, but I was angry at him. How could he talk about her like this? I didn't know what was going on with me. Was I going mad? Why did I care about this girl so much? Was it because she'd rejected me? Or because she was different from the other girls I'd dated? It didn't matter, really; I just wanted to see her again.

When we finished with our breakfast and coffee, Kevin decided to go back to Maggie's house, because he felt tired and dizzy from last night. I told him that I wanted to go for a walk around the town, because I'd never been to Brighton before. He sighed, probably because he was hoping that I would go back to the house and drink with him, but I needed some time alone.

I must have walked around the streets for about two hours, maybe three, thinking about Daniela, when I decided to go to her house and knock on the door. The minute I did, I was sorry, because I didn't know what I was doing or why. I just wanted to see her again.

"You don't give up, do you?"

"Never!"

"So, what is it that you want from me?"

"For you to be my tour guide for one day. I'm not from around here, and I'm sure that you don't want me to get lost, do you?"

"Hmm...I would be glad, actually. Because then I would never see your face again."

"Sure you would. It would be on posters around the whole town, with massive letters on the top, saying MISSING. You don't want to feel guilty because you let me wander around town alone, do you?"

"I can live with that."

"Look, I'm not as bad as you think. Just go out with me. You'll be back by five o'clock, I promise."

"Fine, wait here. I'll be back in five minutes. By the way, what's your name?"

"Ben."

"Surname?"

"Johnson. Why?"

"Because I want to tell my parents who I'm going out with. If something happens to me, they'll know who to blame."

She smiled at me and went back inside the house. I felt my heart jumping and my hands shaking. This was the first time I'd begged a girl to go out with me. My mother used to say that when she met my father, she felt butterflies in her stomach, and she couldn't stop thinking about him. I guess that's what happened to me. If Dad were alive, I would call and ask him for advice.

After ten minutes she came out, wearing blue jeans and a sleeveless yellow top. Her curly brown hair was put up with a few hairpins. This girl had style. She knew exactly what to wear; she looked like one of those models in the fashion magazines. Most of the girls I dated looked like circus clowns, with all those colourful clothes they wore and the makeup they had on their faces. But even though Daniela didn't have a single touch of makeup on, she looked so beautiful.

"So, where do you want to go?" she asked me.

"You're the local girl. You decide."

"Let's go to Preston Park, then."

"You lead."

We walked for about an hour. She didn't stop talking, but I didn't mind. Her voice was soft and tender. She asked me how I'd met Josh, Kevin, and Nigel, about my plans for the future, and many other things.

"I don't like to talk about my family."

"Hmm...strange. OK, I won't ask you anymore. My parents are dentists, and I'm sure you've noticed that I'm not British."

"Yes, I have."

"I came here when I was six. My father decided to move here because he was tired of his job back in Bulgaria. He worked for two years and then signed up for a course at a university and became a dentist. My mother and I came here four years after him. It was difficult in the beginning, because I didn't speak English, and I didn't know anyone. I was used to playing in the street with other children, but I couldn't do that anymore. And I missed my granny."

"I know what you mean. My mother and I moved to London when I was eight. I'm still angry at her."

"But you shouldn't be. I'm sure that she had a reason to do it, and it was for your own good."

"I guess, but she should've asked me first."

"Sometimes people don't have a choice. You were eight. You didn't know what it is not to have money and to take care of a small child. What did you father say when you moved to London?"

"He died two years before that. That's why I'm angry with her. She sold his house and moved to a crappy flat with one bedroom."

"I'm sorry about your father, Ben. Look, when people are desperate, they can do anything. Having an eight-year-old child to take care of on your own and work at the same time is not easy. I was upset when I left my country, but now I understand why my parents made the decision. Trust me, leaving one country and moving to another is more difficult than changing the town you live in. Don't be too harsh on your mother. I'm sure that she's doing the best she can."

"You are so very different from all the girls I've known."

"I really hope so. But you're not like the rest of Maggie's friends. They're idiots, thinking only about sex, drugs, and alcohol. How come you ended up at one of her parties? I know that Josh took you there, but why are you friends with him? You seem pretty smart."

"I can't say that we're what you'd call friends. I don't have friends. Not even Kevin and Nigel. They're just guys I hang out with. I can't count on them when I need help."

"So you are a lonely guy who has lost his way."

"Kind of."

She smiled at me, and I saw her teeth shine like diamonds. I hadn't spoken with someone like this for ages. We walked around the park for hours. She showed me the famous rock garden. Daniela loved nature, because when she was a child, her grandfather used to take her to the woods to pick wild strawberries. She enjoyed every minute of her life—especially when she pushed me into the pond while we were walking on the stepping-stones. I learned a lot about her, and I was right. She was special.

We stopped at a local pizza restaurant and had lunch. Daniela told me that she was studying geology at Imperial College. I wasn't surprised at all, because she surely was intelligent. A smile appeared on my face, because Imperial College was in London, which meant that I had a chance with her.

On our way back, she asked me if I wanted to come with her to the beach. I couldn't say no, because I wanted to spend more time with her. The truth was that I was seriously starting to like her, but I didn't try to kiss her or tell her how I felt. I was scared and, to be honest, I wasn't sure what to do. With the other girls it was easy, but she was different.

"So what are you going to do tonight? Another party?"

"No, I'm planning to go back to London. I don't have anything to do here. Besides, the party last night was boring."

"You're the first person to say that. All the other guys seem to like partying."

"You don't like these parties either."

"Yeah, but I'm not like them."

"According to you, I'm not like them either."

"Are you trying to be smart?"

"I am smart."

"If you say so. Let's go back. It's time for dinner."

I didn't want to take her home. I wanted to spend more time with her, but a promise is a promise, and I planned to keep mine. I asked her if I was going to see her again. She smiled and gave me a piece of paper with her phone number on it.

"Bye, Ben. It was a pleasure being your tour guide for the day."

"I'll return the favour when we go out in London."

"I'll count on that." She smiled at me.

I turned around, but as I was leaving, I heard her calling me. "Oh, and Ben, please be nice to your mother. She sounds like a nice person, and I'm sure that she cares about you. Besides, she's the only one you have left."

"I will try."

"I'll see you in London, then. Bye!"

"Bye, Daniela."

I went back to Maggie's house to get my bag and tell the guys that I was going back to London. I was sure that they wouldn't understand, but I didn't much care. Kevin asked me if I was mad, leaving on Saturday night. Nigel didn't seem to care, and Josh was too busy snogging Maggie.

It was around nine o'clock when I got home. My mother was in the kitchen, preparing dinner. She jumped when she saw me, because she didn't expect me, especially on a Saturday evening. I took my bag to my room and then sat at the table in the dining room.

"Ben, where have you been? I was worried."

"Brighton. But I'm here now, so don't worry."

"I didn't know if you were dead or alive. Your phone was switched off."

"I'm sorry about that."

She looked puzzled. I guess that's because, for the first time in many years, I hadn't shouted at her. And the tone of my voice was friendly, rather than harsh.

"Are you going to have dinner at home, or you are going out?"

"Yes, here, I'm starving."

"I'll bring a plate to your room once dinner is ready."

"Actually, I want to eat here with you."

"OK, who are you, and what have you done with my son?"

"Look, Mum, I know that I've treated you very badly the last few years. I blamed you for everything, but that wasn't right. It was all my fault. I'm sorry. Can you forgive me?"

At first she looked confused, as if she didn't understand what I'd said to her. She stood by the hot plate and stirred the tomato-and-carrot soup. She didn't say a word. After a few minutes, she sat on the chair next to mine and took my hand in hers. "Of course, honey!"

"Let's talk. We haven't done that in ages."

We talked for hours. She told me about Stephen—how they'd met and how difficult it was for her to tell me and introduce him to me. I asked her to tell me how she'd felt when she met my father. I always loved to listen to that story, and especially now, when I had my own story to tell.

I went back to my room after dinner, and I realised that all the anger—all the pain and rage I kept inside my heart—was gone. That night I slept peacefully for the first time since my father died.

CHAPTER 6

It was May 2007, and the sun was shining, which was unusual for that time of the year. I woke up early in the morning, around seven o'clock, got dressed, and left the flat without having breakfast. I'd decided to drop out of college, and I had to go there to fill in the documentation. My mother was not happy with my decision, but she supported me anyway. I didn't see the point of studying, since I had no interest in doing it. She fought with me for three days, but in the end, I convinced her that it was not a good idea to spend her money for nothing.

Besides, she needed this money for the wedding. Stephen had proposed to her. Even though I missed my father and couldn't imagine Mum with another man, I was happy for her. I understood how lonely she had felt all these years. She deserved some happiness. She moved in with him a week after the proposal. She paid the rent for our flat for three months, which was long enough for me to find a job.

"So your mum is getting married?"

"She is. In September."

"Are you excited?"

"Kind of. It's going to be a small ceremony with their closest friends and family."

"How is your job hunting going?"

"I found something. I'll be working as a painter at a refurbishment company."

"That's great! See, I told you that you'd find something. When is your first day?"

"Next Monday."

"But don't forget that you still owe me a tour around London."

"How can I forget? You remind me every time I call you. I'm just waiting for you to get here."

"Well, I'm done with the exams. I have to go to the college on Friday to get a student confirmation letter, but I'll be done by noon."

"I'll call you on Thursday, then."

"Sure. Ben, I have to go now. It's dinnertime. Talk to you soon. Take care."

"You, too. Good night, Daniela."

It had been a month since I'd last seen her in Brighton. She'd given me her phone number, and I texted her the next day. After that I called her, and we spoke about stupid things like football matches. The funny thing was that we could argue forever about which football team performed better: Arsenal or Tottenham. I know that it was strange for an Arsenal fan to fall in love with a Tottenham fan, but I did. We talked about what she liked, her plans for the future, her studies, friends, and many other things. I wanted to know everything about this girl. The more I got to know her, the stronger my feelings for her were growing.

I called Daniela on Thursday evening. She told me that she could meet me at noon the next day at the Westminster tube station. I couldn't believe that I was going to see her again. What was more important was that this was our first date. I can't explain with words how excited—and at the same time how worried—I was. I had no idea where to take her, or what to do, because I had never been on a date. I actually asked my mother for advice. She started laughing before she realised that I was serious. I was sure that my mum never expected me to come to her for help with a girl. But she was happy that I valued her opinion and helped me to plan the whole day anyway. Of course there was a catch. I had to take Daniela for dinner at their house.

Daniela came out of the tube station, and when she saw me, she smiled and hugged me. My heart jumped for a second when she gave me a kiss on each cheek She wore a pink dress with purple roses embroidered on it. I have to admit that the girl had style. Her curls were caught with hairpins on both sides, revealing her round, pale face. She wasn't wearing makeup, and still she was so beautiful that she took my breath away every time I looked at her.

"You look great in that dress!"

"Thanks! I love pink."

"How old are you—five?"

"Ha-ha, very funny! Think pink, babe. That's my motto."

"I will remember that."

"I've got two tickets for the London Eye. I didn't know what your plans were, but I really want to get on the Eye. I've never been on it."

"London Eye? Hmm…OK, let's go."

She took my hand. We walked, holding hands, to pick up the tickets she had bought online. My hands were shaking, but not because she was standing next to me. They were shaking because I was afraid of heights. Once we got on the London Eye, my face grew pale, and I got dizzy from the Eye's movement. I didn't want to look down, so I sat on the bench inside the capsule while Daniela took pictures. She was too excited and busy going around the capsule to notice that I was acting strange. But once we reached the top, she turned to me to ask me to come and take a picture with her. Then she saw that there was something wrong with me.

"Ben, are you OK?"

"Yes. I'm…OK. Don't worry."

"You don't look well. What's wrong? You look like you've just seen a ghost."

"Maybe I did."

"Yes, you did. That's you. Look at your face." She took a small mirror out of her purse and gave it to me. I really did look like a ghost, and I was sweating.

"I think that he's afraid of heights, love," said a man in the capsule. "My son has the same problem."

"Oh, Ben, why didn't you tell me?" But I couldn't reply, because I felt like someone was squeezing my lungs. I couldn't believe what I'd done to myself.

"Ben, are you OK? Answer me!"

"Don't worry, love, he'll be fine in ten minutes."

"What should I do with him? He looks like he's gonna faint."

"Just sit next to him, tell him to look down, with his eyes closed, and hold his hand. He'll be fine."

"Thank you, sir!"

When we got off the London Eye, I ran to the first rubbish bin and threw up in it. I felt so embarrassed. I should never have got on the thing. But how could I say no to her? Daniela came up and gave me a bottle of Evian.

"Here. Drink it. Oh, and you can wash your face with it too. I think you'll feel better."

"Thanks."

"Why didn't you tell me that you were afraid of heights?"

"You looked so excited. I didn't want to disappoint you."

"Oh, you are so cute! If you hadn't just thrown up, I would kiss you. But seriously, don't do that again, OK?"

"OK, I promise. Let's go now. I don't want people to stare at me."

"You deserve it. My mum used to say that the worst things that happen in our lives are caused by us, not others."

"She is so right. Let's go."

After I felt better, and the colour returned to my face, we went for the longest walk I've ever had. First I showed her the Battle of

Britain Monument, which is opposite the London Eye. I told her everything about my father, or at least what I remembered about him.

Time passed quickly while we walked around the Westminster area. We took a picture of the two of us in front of Cupid at Piccadilly Circus. Daniela said that she'd been there many times, but never as a tourist. She climbed on one of the lions at Trafalgar Square, pretending that she was riding it, screaming, "I'm on the top of the world." I couldn't stop laughing, especially when she asked me to help her down, because she couldn't jump.

We visited the London Dungeon, and Daniela held my hand the whole time, even though she laughed at the stories throughout the tour. I think that she only got scared after she heard the story of Jack the Ripper, which is why I took her to Whitechapel after we'd taken pictures in front of Tower Bridge and taken a walk down the riverside. She loved the small, paved Shad Street, which reminded her of the beautiful streets in Verona. I've never been to Italy, but the way she spoke about it made me want to visit.

Daniela and I took a train from London Bridge to Greenwich, which was our last stop for the day before the dinner with my mum and Stephen. I chose to show her this place last, not only because it was one of my favourites, but because it was near Brockley, where Stephen's house was. Daniela was impressed with the view from the observatory. I will never forget her posing in front of the iron globe, at the border between the two hemispheres. She stood with her right leg on the west side and put her right hand on the east side of the line, which indicated where the Greenwich meridian was, while her left hand and leg were in the air. Her body was bent, and it was very difficult for her to keep her balance. I was hardly able to see her face. Then she looked at me and smiled. She couldn't hold this pose for more than ten seconds, and I had to take the picture very fast. She was crazy, but I loved her.

My mum had chicken Caesar salad for a starter, roast beef with mashed potatoes and peas for the main course, and my favourite—apple-and-strawberry pie—for dessert. I was worried that Daniela would feel awkward, but she fit in even better than I did in this setting.

"It must have been very difficult to get into Imperial College."

"To be honest, it was, Caroline, but when I want to achieve something, I don't give up easily."

"I wish Ben was like that."

"But he is. You should've seen him a few months ago when he knocked on my door. He wouldn't take no for an answer."

"I can imagine. It's getting very late. How are you going to get home?"

"Actually, she's staying at my place tonight, Mum."

"Oh, OK. Are you going to a nightclub tonight, then?"

"No, there's just one more place I would like to show her, and then we are going home."

"I'm not a fan of nightclubs, to be honest."

"But why? You're young. You should be partying all night."

"I do, just not here. Every time I go back to Bulgaria, I party for a month and then come back here and study. I don't have much time to do that here."

Daniela and my mum talked all night. Stephen and I watched them without saying a word. "This is what usually happens when you have two women in one place," Stephen whispered to me.

Mum invited her to the wedding. Daniela was so happy that she almost jumped out of her chair. She said it would be her first wedding ever. We left the house at ten thirty and headed to the last place I wanted to show her. I was sure that she would love it, because she'd told me how she missed looking down on her hometown from a cliff. This place was not in the forest, and it wasn't as quiet and dark as it must be in her town, but you could still see half the city from there, with all the lights flickering in the night.

"Close your eyes, now, and hold my hand."

"OK, but please don't leave me, because I will fall on the ground."

"I won't, trust me. Come on."

I held her hand, and we moved very slowly up the stairs of Alexandra Palace. We walked down the terrace and passed by the pub I used to go to with Kevin and Nigel. Once we reached the handrail of the terrace, I told her to open her eyes.

"Where are we?"

"At Alexandra Palace, one of the highest places in London. What do you think?"

"It's...amazing. Look at all the lights. Oh, there's the Swiss Tower, and that's Canary Wharf, isn't it?"

"Yes. I thought that you'd love it, because you were feeling nostalgic. I can't take you to Bulgaria, but at least you can pretend that you are there now."

"My town is a hundred times smaller than London, but I still love this view. Thanks."

She turned to me and looked into my eyes. I was still holding her hand. I thought how beautiful she looked in the moonlight. Her green eyes shone like emeralds, her skin was so white and soft, and her lips were as rose as a pink gerbera. At that moment I told myself that I would never meet anyone like her. She was one of a kind, and I was lucky to have met her. Then I kissed her for the first time.

CHAPTER 7

The days went so fast after I started work that I didn't realise it was September until I saw the leaves falling. I would wake up every morning at five o'clock and go to work five days a week. I had only the weekends off. Daniela would come over to see me, or I would go to Brighton. Even though she slept at my place many times, we didn't have sex. I slept on the sofa in the living room on the night of our first date, and she slept in my bed. But the next time she came to London, Daniela insisted that I sleep with her in the bed, because she couldn't sleep well in new places, and she needed someone to talk to. I'd met her parents at her birthday party in July. They seemed like nice people, and they were very hospitable. I tried some traditional Bulgarian dishes, such as battered feta cheese and meatball soup. Daniela's mother was a great cook.

Daniela and I talked on the phone almost every day. I was so happy. I definitely felt lucky to have her. I never thought that a girl like Daniela would fall in love with me, but she did. She changed my life. I had been heading down a path from which there would be no return, but she showed me the right way. She helped me realise that I had better options than selling drugs and getting drunk. If I kept doing that, eventually I would go to prison. Daniela also helped me realise what I had done to my mother, how I'd made her feel, and how to fix my relationship with her before it was too late. That's why I loved her so much. She was always there for me when I needed her. I have to admit that she was the smart one in our relationship.

When Kevin and Nigel found out that I was dating Daniela, they started to make fun of me. They called me names, such as "pussy" and "the henpecked man," because I respected my girlfriend and her opinion. Kevin said that I was an idiot because I had a decent job. He told me that it was stupid to work like a dog and go home tired and spent. I could've chosen the easy life Josh offered us. But I didn't care what they thought about me. I knew what was right for me, and what I had to do with my life. They were just a bunch of bozos whose lives were meaningless. I couldn't believe that I used to call those worms my friends. I stopped talking to them a few weeks after the party at Maggie's house. They kept calling me, though, asking if I was interested in going to another party with the so-called gang they were in. But I wasn't, and I always said no when they called. Soon Nigel and Kevin stopped with the phone calls and broke off all contact with me. The only good thing that came out of our friendship was that I met Daniela.

Four days before my mother's wedding, I still didn't have a suit. Daniela had bought her dress a few days after my mother invited her to the ceremony. I don't know why, but she took me shopping with her, even though her best friend, Karisha, came with us as well. I didn't know the meaning of the word "madness" until the day I went shopping with those two. They ran from one shop to another until Daniela found the dress of her dreams. We must have visited at least twenty shops and spent six hours walking around Oxford Street. At the very last shop, she found her dress. Both Karisha and I agreed that Daniela looked amazing in it. I have to admit that this dress was womanly and stylish. It was pale pink in colour, with one shoulder, and it was slightly above her knees. But what made it unique was the white overskirt that reached her ankles and was tied in a delicate rose at her waist. Daniela and Karisha had stopped asking if I liked one dress or another after the fifth shop we visited, because they knew that I was only trying to stop their shopping by saying I liked them all. But when Daniela saw my jaw drop when she came out of the changing room wearing the pink dress, she knew instantly that she had to buy it.

The same madness started over again when we had to look for a suit for me, four days before the wedding. I really wanted to buy the first one I saw, just to get it over with, but Daniela wouldn't let me. Karisha agreed with her. Daniela said that I was her Ken doll and she wanted to have some fun dressing me up in different styles of suits. God, I must have loved her more than I thought, to let her torture me like that.

"It's going to be a small ceremony!" I insisted, but they didn't listen to a word I said.

"It doesn't matter. It's your mum's wedding."

"Oh, my dear Lord, what did I do to you to deserve this for a second time?"

"Do you hate us, Ben?"

"To be honest, Karisha, right now I do!" I smiled at her, because she obviously thought that I was serious. "I'm just joking. I love you both, but if you make me go to another shop, I swear to God, I will push you both down the escalator!"

"Try this one, and we are done, I promise." How could I have said no to Daniela? I loved her smile and the look in her eyes when she was excited.

"Fine, torture me for half an hour more, and then we are done. Do we have a deal?"

"Yes, we do. Now try this one, Ken."

I wasn't happy that they were having so much fun watching me try on one suit after another, but I was helpless. One guy against two girls was not a fair fight. Daniela and Karisha chose a dark grey suit for me. Daniela thought that the white shirt Karisha chose was too conservative and picked a light blue one. They finished the look by adding a silver tie. To my surprise, I was actually pleased with their choice. But I was even more pleased that my torture was finally over.

The ceremony was held in a small chapel in Brockley. Daniela helped my mum with the decoration of the hall. My mother asked her for help with the preparations because she didn't have many friends who could help her. Besides, she liked Daniela and wanted to make her feel like part of the family. She was grateful that Daniela was the reason I had changed and continued my life without any drugs, fights, or a criminal record.

The benches were decorated with white lilies, and the altar had two vases that held purple and white tulips. There weren't many guests, probably around forty—family members, friends from the universities they had attended, colleagues from the hospital, and my grandparents. Since my mum's parents were not among the living, she felt Grandma and Grandpa were like her own. She'd kept up her relationship with them after my father's death, because she respected and loved them. They sat next to Daniela and me. I introduced her to them before the ceremony. Grandma was impressed and surprised that that I had found a girl who was polite, smart, and beautiful. She was also glad that Daniela was leading me down the right path.

When I saw my mother walk to the altar in her long, white dress, her hair tight in a bun, smiling nervously, I felt so proud of her. She had got over her husband's death. She gave up everything to take care of her son, even though it wasn't easy. And there she was, standing next to her new husband, having finally found her happiness.

After the ceremony, we all went to the hotel where the reception was held. First we had champagne on the terrace, where Stephen and Mum cut the wedding cake. Stephen's best mate gave a speech about what a great couple they were. He made a few jokes about the parties they'd attended at university. He ended with a few words about the marriage and their happiness.

When we got to the restaurant for the dinner party, I couldn't help but notice what a great job the coordinator had done. There were white chair covers, and yellow ribbons tied on the back of each chair. Silver candelabras with three candles had been placed on each table, and bright-yellow rose petals in the shape of a heart were spread around them. Everything was lovely, including the food. I'd never tasted anything as delicious as the chocolate soufflé that was served for dessert.

My mother had asked me to make a speech after the dinner. It was tough to prepare a whole speech, especially when writing was not one of my best skills. I struggled when I started writing it; I didn't know how to begin. I didn't want to make it funny. I wanted it to be serious and honest. But what I could say? Something like, "I treated my mother like trash for eleven years. I hated her, I hated the groom, but hey, now I'm here, and I'm happy for them." Luckily I had Daniela to help me with the writing. She told me that I had to stop punishing myself for what I'd done. It was in the past. What mattered was that my mum was getting married, and I had the honour of making a speech at the party.

"Dear guests, I would like to thank you all for coming to my mother and Stephen's wedding. I'm not good at speeches, but my mum asked me to do it, and I couldn't refuse. How can you say no to this lovely woman, after all? Dear Mum, I know that we've had our ups and downs, but I love you, and I'm grateful that you finally found your happiness, just as I've found mine. Stephen, I have to admit that I wasn't charmed by the idea that someone else was going to join our family at first, but I realised how much you love my mother. And now I would like to welcome you to our family! I wish you both a strong marriage, full of love and unforgettable moments. Be there for each other, no matter what difficulties life puts in your way. Everybody, please raise your glass. For Mum and Stephen!"

All the guests raised their glasses full of champagne and said, "For Caroline and Stephen!" When I sat down, Mum looked at me and smiled. She didn't say anything, but I saw the gratitude in her eyes. Daniela took my hand under the table and kissed me on my right cheek.

"So when you said that you've found your happiness, what did you mean?"

"Don't pretend you don't know."

"Hmm...do I?"

"Why are you girls always like this?"

"Maybe because we want hear something, even though we know it."

"You are my happiness, Daniela."

I saw the sparkle in her eyes. I knew that it wasn't only from the two glasses of champagne she'd had, but from all the love coming from her heart. I hadn't thought that I would find someone who would love me so much, because I hadn't believed in love until I met Daniela.

After few hours of dancing, laughter, and two funny speeches from Stephen and mum's friends, we decided to leave. My mum and Stephen stayed at the hotel because they were leaving for the airport the next morning. They were going to spend their honeymoon in Dubai. Mum had always wanted to go there, and she was so happy when Stephen bought the tickets and booked a five-star hotel for the week.

"I have to find a place to stay here in London, because I won't be able to travel to Brighton every day. We have lectures three days a week, and I have to go to the practical exercises, which are two days a week. I will be very busy this year."

"Why don't you come and live with me? You won't be paying rent, and we can spend more time together."

"I don't know. I have to think about it. I'm not sure that my parents would approve."

"I will speak with them. I'm sure that they wouldn't mind. At least you won't be alone. They don't have to be worried about you."

"We'll see. Do you mind if I take off my shoes? My feet are tired."

"Take off your shoes? Are you serious?"

"Deadly."

She took off her shoes and walked barefoot. She looked so short without her shoes. I was worried that she might get hurt, so I decided to carry her to my place, which was only two hundred meters away. Daniela laughed when I lifted her. She didn't stop talking until we reached the front door. I had to put her down to open the door.

Daniela went to the bathroom to wash her feet, and I changed from my fancy suit into comfortable pyjamas in the bedroom. She came into the room. I asked her if she wanted me to leave so she could put her nightgown on, but she said that it was fine—we were about to live together, after all.

Even though I stayed in the room, I turned around because I didn't want to disturb her privacy. Daniela got in bed and turned so she could see my face.

"So, how do you feel after the wedding?"

"Tired. I just want to sleep now."

"Hug me first, and then you can sleep."

I hugged her, and we stayed like that for a while. I didn't want to let her go. I wanted to feel her next to me. I wanted to hold her like this forever. I had to do my best to convince her parents to let her stay at my place instead of living alone. I wanted to see her every day, to be next to her every night. I wanted to be with her forever.

Daniela looked into my eyes. She stroked my face and then she kissed me. I kissed her back. I gave her a kiss on the neck. I felt her shaking, but I didn't stop. I kissed her tenderly and fondled her body. She looked at me with her emerald eyes. The same sparkle I saw at the wedding flashed for a second. I asked her if she was sure that she wanted this. I didn't want her to do something she would regret, because I knew how important it was for her. She would remember her first time all her life. Daniela nodded. I smiled. Then I got on top of her and started kissing her all over her body. I took her nightgown off and held her in my arms. She was so small, so fragile. I asked if she was OK. I knew that I had to be very gentle. I was so scared that I might hurt her. I felt her breath on my skin, her touch. My heart jumped like mad every time her lips touched my body. Her scent was sweet and unforgettable. Her kisses were timid and uncertain.

When it was over, I took her in my arms and kissed her. My heart was bursting. I knew that I was the luckiest man in the world to have her only for myself. I whispered in her ear, "I love you!"

CHAPTER 8

Daniela moved in with me two weeks after my mother's wedding. It wasn't easy to convince her parents to let her live with me. It took us days, because she was their only child, and they were not ready to let her go. The truth was that they didn't want to accept the fact that she was eighteen already. In the end, she managed to convince them that it was better to live with me than to be alone and pay rent.

I had to rent a car to help Daniela with her luggage. I thought that a small person like her would not have a lot of bags, but I was wrong. She came out of the door carrying an enormous bag, and her dad followed her with two suitcases that were taller than she was. I hit my head with my right hand and wondered how the bloody hell I was going to carry all those suitcases to the third floor, where my flat was, without a lift. She looked at me and said, "What? I am a woman! Did you actually expect that I would show up with fewer than two suitcases?"

Our relationship was great so far. After the first night we'd spent together, I felt like the happiest guy in the world. There were not many girls like her, who enjoyed life as she did, who had goals and knew exactly how to achieve them.

After Daniela's lectures started, we didn't have much time to spend together, because she would come home very late, and she was too tired to do anything. The only thing she did was to take a shower and have dinner before going to bed. I, on the other hand, learned to cook, and I would wait for her every night with a different meal. The only days we had to ourselves were Saturday and Sunday, which we would spend with my mum and Stephen or with her parents. Sometimes she would go to Brighton on her own, and I would watch movies all night at home.

At the end of September, I decided to take her to my favourite park—Bruce Castle Park—to show her the biggest and oldest oak tree I'd ever seen. It was more than three hundred years old. We had a picnic under it. Even though it was September, the weather was hot, and we wanted to stay in its shadow. At one point Daniela got really hot. She went to the children's swimming pool to cool herself. I laughed because she was no taller than a twelve-year-old child. She was a child herself, and that was one of the things I loved most about her. When we sat back on the blanket after her baby-pool experience, Daniela took a picture of me taking a bite of one of the sandwiches she'd made before we left the flat. She said that she would upload it to Facebook so that everyone could see how hungry I was. She used to do that often. Taking pictures when I was least expecting it was one of her favourite things. I grabbed the camera from Daniela's hands and took a picture of her holding an oak leaf. I will never forget that day, because it was one of the happiest of my life.

Time passed so fast that I barely realised when December came. I had to take a two-week holiday for Christmas and New Year, because Daniela wanted us to spend Christmas with her family. It was her favourite holiday, so I had to choose the perfect present for her. And since she wanted to go for dinner with her parents on Christmas Eve, I accepted my mum's invitation for lunch on Christmas Day. It was a tradition in Daniela's family to open the presents after dinner on Christmas Eve.

I went to Ernest Jones with Karisha a few days before the dinner, because I had no idea what to buy for Daniela. I already knew that her father liked ship model kits, so I went to a lovely shop in Croydon, where my father used to take me when I was a kid. It must have been a very successful shop, because it had been there for more than fifteen years. It was run by an old man, who used to give me a lollipop every time I went there. That was because Dad used to buy a lot of aeroplane models, which we would put together whenever he was home. The man sold puzzles and other things, such as ships in bottles and battleship kits. I chose the whaling ship, *Charles W. Morgan*, which was an American ship from 1841. Daniela had told me that her mum loved tapestry sewing, so I chose a beautiful winter landscape tapestry kit for her. I'd planned to buy chocolates and wine for the dinner, but Daniela told me that her parents were abstaining and the dinner was Lenten.

Karisha and I became close after I started dating Daniela. She would come to our place almost every day. The three of us had dinner, lunch, or just watched a movie. That was the reason I asked her for help choosing a gift for Daniela. She struggled with the idea at first, but then she remembered how much Daniela had loved Mrs Frost's snowflake necklace when we watched *Batman and Robin*, starring George Clooney and Arnold Schwarzenegger. We checked online, and the one I liked most was from Ernest Jones. And they were able to engrave it, though there was not much space on the back. I asked them to engrave her name only. We bought a small gift box, where I put the necklace, along with the snowflake charm. I made a personalised card, with her face on Snow White's body and mine on Rudolf's. Karisha laughed when she saw the card, because I'd ordered it from an online store for personalised gifts. I was sure that Daniela would love it.

On Christmas Eve, we got dressed and prepared ourselves for the dinner at Daniela's parents'. I made sure that we didn't forget anything, because she tended to forget or lose things. She said it was because she had to think about so many things. I took all the presents and put them in the car. She was always late and always in a hurry. Sometimes I would get very pissed while I waited for her, but she would smile at me and say, "Sorry, love." I always forgot all my frustration and anger the moment I saw her smile.

We were late for dinner, thanks to Daniela. Luckily her mum knew her daughter very well and was not surprised. Even though I'd known her parents for quite a while now, I didn't feel comfortable with them. Parents were not my specialty. They were nice to me and trusted me with their daughter, because they were confident that I would take care of her, but I burned with shame when I was with them. I couldn't just call them Mary and Chris, although they asked me to; I called them sir and ma'am.

However, during this dinner I felt like part of their family. I hadn't known how different from ours their culture and traditions were. They served different kinds of fresh fruit, dried fruit, nuts, some kind of bean dish, rice wrapped in grape leaves, and homemade bread with a coin inside. I was told that whoever found the coin would be lucky, happy, healthy, and wealthy for the whole year. I wasn't the lucky one, Daniela's mum was, but I had fun digging into my piece of bread.

After we finished dinner, Daniela headed straight to the Christmas tree, where all the presents were stacked. When I asked her if she was going to help her mum with the table, she told me that their tradition said that all the dishes should be left on the table so that Jesus could eat from them, too. It sounded really strange to me, but I went and sat next to her. She passed out all the presents to their recipients and hurried to unwrap hers.

"Thanks for the Kindle, Mum, because I'm sure that you chose it…and Dad, because you paid for it, didn't you? I love it! I can keep all the articles I like and read them on my way to uni now."

"Well, we thought it was a great idea. Ben, the tapestry is wonderful. Thank you, but you shouldn't have. I appreciate it."

"You are welcome, Mrs Ivanova."

"Ben, it's amazing! Where did you find it? It's exactly the same!"

"Well, not exactly, but it looks like it."

"Shut up! I love it, thanks! And it's got my name engraved on the back."

She kissed my cheek and went back to opening her presents. Her father loved the ship, and I received two extremely useful presents from Daniela's parents—a Victorinox Swiss Army knife and a rescue tool. Since I worked on building sites, both would come in handy. Daniela's present for me was a silver, engraved picture frame, saying "I love you, Ben!" at the bottom, with the picture I'd taken at Bruce Castle Park the day we had our picnic. She looked so beautiful in this picture, with her bright smile, rosy lips, and curly brown hair, an oak leaf in her hand.

"Look at the back of the frame." When I did, I saw the same picture, but smaller and laminated. There was something written on the back of it in her handwriting. "Admit it—you love me. 'cause maybe...I love you, too. ☺ Of course I love you, silly! Never forget that."

"This one is for your wallet. I knew that you wanted a picture, but instead of giving you my crappy passport photo, I decided to give you this one, because I look good in it. Oh, and I've left you a kiss on the back, so that you don't forget how sweet my lips are." She whispered the last sentence, because she was afraid that her parents would hear. She kissed my cheek again.

"Oh look, it's midnight. You have to make a wish!" I didn't know what to wish for. I had everything I wanted. I just wanted everything to stay this way. My life was finally getting better, and I was happy.

We all had a glass of red wine and went to bed. I had to sleep in the guest room, and Daniela slept in her room. Even though we'd been living together for three months, we had to sleep in separate rooms every time we visited her parents. I have to admit that if I had a daughter, I would have wanted the same, and to be honest, I would never have let her live with her boyfriend unless they were married.

Daniela woke me up the next morning. When we went downstairs, the table had already been cleared away from last night, and there was a warm breakfast there waiting for us. A few hours later, we were on our way to Stephen's house for Christmas lunch with my relatives—and Stephen's, of course. He was part of our family now.

Mum had all my favourite foods on the table. I asked Daniela to stay close to me, because my relatives could get very nosy and annoying. Besides, I knew that Stephen's place would turn into a crazy house. Poor him, I'm sure that he didn't know what he was getting into, even though he got part of the picture on their wedding day.

"Ben, can you come here for a moment, please?"

"Yes, Mum, what is it?"

"I have to tell you something—actually we have to tell you something—but I don't know how you are going to react." Stephen was standing behind her, with his hands on her shoulders.

"You're scaring me. Is there something wrong with you? Are you sick?"

"Hey, what's up? What's with the worried face?"

"Oh, great, Daniela, you are here, too. There's nothing to be worried about. Everything's fine. I just wanted to tell you that I'm pregnant."

"Congratulations, Caroline! I'm so happy for you." Daniela hugged my mum and kissed her. I stood in front of her, not knowing what to say.

"Mum, you scared me! I thought that you were sick or something."

"Don't just stand there like that. Say something to your mother."

"Oh, I'm sorry, Mum. I was stunned for a moment. Daniela's right, I have to say something. Congratulations, Mum! I hope that you won't have as many problems with this one as you had with me." I smiled and hugged her. It was so strange. I wasn't expecting to have a little brother or sister, but I was happy for her. I couldn't wait for this baby to come into this world. I imagined what it would be like to have my own baby with Daniela. I think that that was the moment I decided that I wanted to marry her and spend the rest of my life with her.

After a long day with my relatives, Daniela and I headed back to our place. On our way home, I couldn't stop thinking about starting a family of our own.

"You're very quiet. What are you thinking about?"

"You."

"Liar!"

CHAPTER 9

It was the beginning of April. Daniela was worried about her upcoming exams. She spent most of her time at the university. We didn't have much time to see each other and talk. I had more time for myself. I would go to the gym every evening. I'd think about whether I was ready to take the next step in our relationship. I knew that things between us were going very fast, but I was sure that I wouldn't find anyone like her. Sometimes I thought she was too good for me, and I didn't know what I'd done to have her next to me.

At the end of each training, I would reach the same conclusion, which was that I had to propose to her and marry her before someone else did, because I would kick myself later for letting her go. That's why I called Karisha on April 5 and asked her for help. She got so excited that she screamed on the phone for five minutes. She said "OMG" more than twenty times. I knew that she was the perfect person to help me with ideas for the proposal and everything, but I was worried that she wouldn't be able to keep it a secret.

"Any plans so far?"

"Nope. That's why I called you. You know me. I'm not romantic, and I'm not good with these things."

"You are so lucky that you've got me, then. I've known Daniela since we were in primary school. I can give you some ideas."

"I'm waiting."

"OK, here's a thought. Why don't you take her for dinner somewhere, put some roses and candles in the living room, and propose to her when you come back?"

"That's a great idea, but we live together. I won't be able to do all the decoration stuff without her noticing. Besides, I'm not good with decorating."

"Fine! Take her for dinner. I'll go to your place after you leave and decorate."

"You're the best!"

"I know. And don't worry. I'll keep it a secret."

"I really hope so. I want to surprise her."

We spent a week planning for the big day. I asked for a few days off. We had to go to buy a ring, choose the perfect restaurant, decide how to decorate the rooms, and of course decide what I was going to say to her, because I wasn't very good at sharing my feelings. I had to tell my mum as well. She didn't seem surprised, but she had to ask me if I was sure. She talked about responsibilities, children, work, and all that family stuff. My mother was concerned that Daniela's parents wouldn't be as happy as I was.

"Sweetheart, don't you think that you should speak with them first?"

"We'll tell them later. I don't think that there will be a problem."

"You are both just nineteen. I have no idea what their traditions are and what they consider an acceptable age to get married."

"We won't get married the next day, Mum. We're gonna wait for a year, at least, until she graduates. Besides, we have to plan everything, and she doesn't have time to do it now."

"I still think that you should think about it some more."

"What is there to think about, Mum? I've decided already. I love her. She makes me happy, and I want to be with her."

"If you are 100 per cent sure that she's the one, then I agree, and I'll be happy for you."

"I am."

My mother agreed with me, although I was sure that she had second thoughts, just as all parents do when they realise that their children are going to have families of their own. I didn't care what she thought. I only wanted to be with the woman I loved and spend the rest of my life with her.

Karisha and I went to H. Samuel in Oxford Street to buy the ring. It was not an easy job. There were so many that I couldn't decide. Americans say that an engagement ring should cost at least three months' salary. As much as I wanted to spend thirty-five hundred pounds for a ring, I couldn't afford it. Besides, Daniela didn't like things just because they were expensive. She liked them because they reminded her of something or someone. I wanted to give her something simple but posh.

"What do you think about this one, Ben?"

"No, I don't like it."

"You don't like anything! We must have seen at least fifteen rings by now."

"I know, I know. But I just can't decide."

"You have to, because we don't have much time. The reservation is for next Friday, and you have to get it engraved as well, so pick one. Let's get over with it, because this is the fifth store we've been in."

"Now you know how I felt when you two dragged me around the shops for suits, dresses, and shoes!"

"OK, I give up."

I knew that Karisha was tired, because she was getting a little bitchy. That always happened when she was hungry and tired. I had to take her for lunch somewhere, or she would kill me. She stood at the exit, waiting for me. And then I saw it. That was it! There it was, in the window display. I called Karisha, and she came into the shop again.

When at first she saw the ring, she was speechless. But after a few seconds she said "That's it! Buy it. It's amazing!"

"I know. How come we didn't notice it before?"

"I have no idea. But Daniela will love it."

"OK, we'll take it."

The ring was made of white gold and had a one-carat diamond, with ten little pink zirconium stones around it in the shape of a heart. Unfortunately it was too big for Daniela's finger, and I had to leave it in the shop for both sizing and engraving.

Karisha was so glad that we'd found a ring that she forgot how hungry she was. I took her to Pizza Hut for lunch, and we discussed the decorations for the apartment. She suggested making a path of red rose petals to the small table in the living room, where the ring would be, and to have red and pink candles all around the room. This idea was a little too much for me, because I wasn't a romantic type of guy, but Daniela was crazy about this stuff. She would cry at every romantic movie, especially at *The Notebook*, her favourite. I was clumsy, and I didn't know how to express my feelings—I mean feelings like love, care, interest. Unfortunately, the only feeling I was able to express perfectly was anger. That's why I left Karisha to do whatever she thought best. She made me feel like an actor playing a part in the next romantic movie hit, by telling me what to say and how to act. I didn't mind, to be honest, because the only thing I wanted was to make Daniela happy. Karisha knew exactly how to do that.

"Where are we going, Ben?"

"You'll see. Just wait. We're almost there."

"Where are you going to park the car in the middle of Piccadilly Circus?"

"Don't worry, I'll find a place."

It was April 20, 2008, a date I will never forget. I parked the car near Leicester Square, and we walked to the restaurant. I knew that she loved sushi, so I had made a reservation at Aqua, a fancy restaurant near the Oxford Street tube station. It was one of her favourite places in London and quite expensive, too. But I wanted to make her feel special.

We arrived at the restaurant early and sat at the bar until they called us. The place was packed, because it was a Friday. Daniela ordered a strawberry daiquiri, her favourite cocktail. I couldn't drink because I was driving, so I ordered a Coke. The hostess called us before we finished our drinks, so we took them with us to our table. I couldn't help noticing how the other guys in the bar stared at Daniela. She was so beautiful that night. I hoped that soon she would become my wife.

"What's with the fancy restaurant tonight?"

"I just wanted to do something special for you."

"I know that our first anniversary is coming up soon. And I assume that you've got more surprises in store."

"You have no idea."

I'd been so busy with the preparations and everything, I'd forgotten that our anniversary was near. For a moment I thought back to the night I kissed her for the first time, and I couldn't believe that it had been a whole year since we got together. So many things had happened during that year.

"Which one do you prefer: tataki sushi or fruit maki?"

"I have no idea what to order, because I don't know what's in it anyway. Just order whatever you like, love."

"Fine. I'll order both, plus the bento box and the king crab tempura."

"I have no idea what you just said, but I'll have noodles."

"You are the only person who goes to a sushi restaurant and orders noodles."

"I'm unique. That's why you love me, isn't it?"

She smiled, showing her perfect teeth, and kissed me. I took that as a yes and kissed her back. We dined for about two hours, and then we had another drink at the bar. I was nervous, and Daniela sensed it.

"Wait, wait, wait!"

"Why? What's wrong?"

"Come here."

I went to her and hugged and kissed her. She told me that she wanted a Hollywood kiss, just like Carrie from *Sex and the City* and that writer guy, whose name I didn't remember (and to be honest, I didn't care). But I gave her what she wanted. I leaned her back and kissed her.

"Ben, there's something I want to give you."

"What is it?" She opened her bag, took out a small box, and gave it to me.

"I found this a few weeks ago in the attic. I didn't know what it was, so I showed it to your mum. She told me that it was a gift from your father."

"It was. I haven't seen it for ages. I thought that I'd lost it somewhere. He bought it for me when I was five. We went to the RAF Museum that day. It was the last time I saw him alive. He went on a mission the next morning and never came back."

"I'm so sorry, Ben. I didn't want to upset you. I was wondering why you've changed your mind. Your mum told me that you wanted to become a pilot. What happened?"

"I was just a child who admired his father. I wanted to be like him, but then he died and left us all alone. I couldn't blame him, because he was dead. I used to blame Mum for everything. That's how I became who I was before I met you. My dream to become a pilot died with my father."

"It's never too late, you know. You can always follow your dreams."

"That's not my dream anymore. I don't want to risk leaving my children and my wife alone."

"Don't be a pessimist! Since you gave up this dream, do you have a new one?"

"You'll find out soon enough."

As we walked to the car park, Daniela kept asking me about my father and my passion for aeroplanes. And for the first time since we'd been together, I was ready to talk about it. She made me remember how much I loved aeroplanes and how passionate I was about them.

Daniela switched on the radio when we got in the car. She would do that every time we were out. She loved to sing, even though she couldn't. She thought that her singing drove me mad, but I loved it. Every time Daniela sang a song, I smiled.

"Oh, that's my favourite! Listen! Listen!"

"I'm listening."

"'And I miss you…like the deserts miss the rain. And I miss you…' Sing with me, Ben! 'And I can almost hear you shout down to me, where I always used to be…'"

"You are crazy."

"I know. 'And I miss you…' Ben, watch out!"

I didn't see the other car coming towards us. It drove on our side of the road. I moved the wheel to the right, but it was too late. Everything happened so fast. I didn't have time to react. The lights of the other car shone in my eyes, and I couldn't see anything. A second later I felt it cut into my Vauxhall. It spun around the road and hit a tree.

When I opened my eyes, I saw that Daniela was unconscious. She was covered with blood. There were pieces of glass on her face and her body. I reached for her hand and checked to see if she had a pulse. She was still alive. The knife her father gave me for Christmas was in my door pocket. I took it and cut my seatbelt with it. When I moved, I felt a pain in my right leg. I saw that there was blood coming from it, but I didn't care. I only wanted to take Daniela out. I cut her seatbelt and dragged her out of the car.

A car stopped. The driver got out and ran to us. His passenger dialled emergency, 999, to call an ambulance. The car that hit us was on the other side of the road, upside down. I didn't know if the driver was still alive, and I didn't care. The man who called the ambulance asked me something, but I was too weak to answer.

The ambulance came a few minutes later. Two medics came to me. They were saying things I didn't understand. A third one came with a stretcher. I knew that they would put me on it, but first they had to make sure that it was safe for me to be moved. I held Daniela's hand. When they lifted me, I whispered, "No."

They placed her on the stretcher and slid her inside the second ambulance. I heard someone talking. I didn't know who it was. A voice behind me said that they had to be very careful with the girl. I lifted my hand, but the nurse next to me told me that I had to stay still. I wanted to scream Daniela's name, but I couldn't say anything because of the mask on my face. I wanted to be with her. I wouldn't stop moving, and the nurse injected me with something. A few seconds later, I lost consciousness.

CHAPTER 10

I woke up in a hospital room. I didn't remember the car accident. There was no one else in the room. I was alone. And then it all came back to me. I wanted to call someone. There was a sharp pain in my head. I couldn't move, because I was tied to so many machines. I couldn't speak, because there was a mask on my face. I lay there, feeling hopeless. I didn't know if Daniela was alive.

A few minutes later a nurse came into the room. I couldn't see her face properly, because my eyes were blurry. She asked me something, but I couldn't hear what she said. She left the room. I was nervous. I wanted to move. I couldn't understand why I didn't feel anything, why I wasn't able to control my arms or legs.

The nurse came back with a doctor. His face looked familiar. My sight got better, and I realised where I was. I was at Middlesex Hospital, where my mum used to work. The man standing next to my bed was Dr Rashid. I knew him and his wife, because they used to have dinner at our place from time to time. He came up to my bed and took something that looked like a pen from his pocket. Dr Rashid opened my left eye and pointed the pen at it. I saw a light coming out of it, and for a second I felt as if I was blind and couldn't see anything. He did the same with my right eye. Then he moved away from my face.

"Your reactions are pretty good, Ben. Do you want me to remove the respirator?"

I nodded. The only thing I wanted—more than knowing what had happened to Daniela—was to get rid of that thing and ask all the questions I had in my mind. Once the tube was out, he told me not to speak for a while and to breathe normally. I smelled the hospital odours, all the unpleasant scents of drugs and bleach, but I was happy to be alive. But I couldn't stop thinking about Daniela. Had she survived?

"How do you feel, Ben?"

"Like a smashed frog on the road."

I heard my voice, but I didn't recognize it. It sounded so strange, like a little roar. I wondered how long I had been asleep.

"Where's Mum?"

"She spent the night here, but Stephen took her home. She needs rest because of the baby. I can call her, if you want me to."

"That's OK. What day is it?"

"It's Sunday. You were unconscious for two days. I have to check your limbs' reactions, if you don't mind."

"Where's Daniela? Is she OK?"

"Let me check your reactions first. Tell me if you feel anything."

He grabbed a small needle and pricked my left heel. It felt ticklish. Then Dr Rashid did the same with my right heel. I knew that there was something wrong with Daniela. I felt it. He didn't want to give me any information about her, which meant that she wasn't doing well.

"Dr Rashid, can you please tell me where Daniela is? Is she OK?"

"Ben, you should have some rest now."

"I've had enough rest. I want to see her."

I tried to stand, but I wasn't even able to sit. When I lifted my head from the pillow, I felt dizzy and sick. The nurse pushed me back down on the bed, which made me feel even worse. I threw up on the floor.

"I told you to stay calm, Ben! Give him some water, Nurse."

"I just want to know about Daniela. Please, Dr Rashid, tell me. I need to know!"

"Ben, I'm sorry, but Daniela didn't make it. The doctors did their best, but she didn't survive. Her lung was damaged very badly. She lost a lot of blood. They couldn't stop the internal bleeding. I'm so sorry, Ben."

I think that my heart stopped for a second. I didn't want to believe that she was gone, that I was never going to see her again. When my heart started beating again, I felt the pain. It was worse than anything I had felt in my life. I wanted to take a knife and stab myself to make it stop. I stood up. I pulled off all the monitors and IVs and screamed.

"Nurse, hold him. He must not move. Call someone, fast. We need to calm him down."

I heard Rashid's shouts and felt his hands on me, but he couldn't hold me. Two attendants were waiting for me outside the door. They held me while Rashid injected something in me. I felt sleepy and sank into the attendants' arms.

That was the last thing I remembered from that day. I woke up the next morning and saw my mum holding my hand. She looked worried, and from the look of her red cheeks, I could tell that she had cried all night.

"Mum…"

"Hey, you're awake. Don't move. Just stay in bed. Do you need something? I can get it for you."

"I want to see her."

"Oh, honey, you know that you can't. You have to stay in bed for a few days."

"I have to see her for the last time, Mum. I have to say good-bye."

"Ben, she's not here. She was taken back to Bulgaria. Her parents didn't want her to be buried here."

"It's all my fault. I was driving the car. I was supposed to protect her, to keep her safe."

"No, honey, it wasn't your fault. The other driver was drunk. You couldn't do anything to save her. We're lucky that you survived."

"I should've died, not her!"

"Calm down, Ben!"

"Don't tell me to calm down. You don't know how I feel!"

"I don't? Are you forgetting something? I know what it is to lose someone you love. I know what it is to kiss that person good-bye and pray every day that he'll be safe. Don't tell me that I don't know how you feel."

"You didn't kill him, but I killed her. I killed her."

"No, Ben, you didn't kill her. The man who hit you killed her. He almost killed you as well."

"What's going to happen with him?"

"He's dead, Ben. He got what he deserved."

"No, he didn't. He should've gone to prison. Then he'd have to think about what he did for the rest of his life. If he ever forgot, I'd have gone there to remind him."

I turned to the other side, because I didn't want to talk to her anymore. I was angry, furious, because I'd lost the woman I loved, and no one seemed to understand how I felt.

I couldn't believe that she was gone. I was never going to hear her voice again, look into her eyes, or laugh with her. She was never going to sleep next to me, sing along with the radio, or cry on my shoulder. Worst of all, I couldn't even say good-bye to her. I didn't want to go to the funeral. I didn't know how I was going to look into her parents' eyes. How could I explain to them why I didn't save their daughter, why I killed her? It was all my fault. I blame myself for what happened that night every single day of my life.

A few days after I woke up, Daniela's mum came to see me. I was surprised by her visit. I hadn't expected her to come to the hospital. She had so many things to sort for the funeral. I can't say that I wasn't glad to see her, but I was also afraid of what she might want. I didn't want her to blame me, but I was ready to face her rage. She needed to express her feelings, although I knew that this would not help her accept the fact that she was never going to see her daughter again.

The first thing I noticed was that she was dressed in black. Her face reminded me of my mum's at Dad's funeral. She looked different without makeup. I could tell that she had been crying a lot. I could sense her pain, not only because I could see it in her eyes, but because I had the same pain nested in my heart.

"Hello, Ben. How are you?"

"Not very well, Mrs Ivanova, but I can't complain."

"Your mum told me that you woke up a few days ago, and I decided to come to see you."

"Thank you, I appreciate it."

"Ben, why can't you look me in the eyes?"

"What do you mean?"

"You are looking at the wall in front of you. Why can't you look into my eyes, Ben?"

"I...I...No...I'm..."

"You think that it was your fault, don't you?"

"It was. If it wasn't for me, she would be alive."

"Ben, look at me. No one knew what was going to happen. There are things in life that can't be explained. It wasn't your fault that a foolish man decided to get drunk and caused a car crash. He was the one who killed her, not you."

"But I couldn't save her!"

"No one could, darling. Her injuries were too extensive. She never woke up."

She paused for a moment, and I felt her grief. It was extremely difficult for her to talk about the accident in which she had lost her only daughter. I saw a tear coming from her left eye, one that she couldn't stop from falling. I felt even worse, because Mary was a great woman, and I had caused both her and her husband pain, which they would never get over.

"You should know, Ben, that we don't blame you for what happened. At first I was angry at you, because I left my daughter in your care, and now she's gone. But after a few days, I realised that you couldn't have done anything to save her. I don't blame you,

Ben. Don't feel sorry for yourself. Don't spend the rest of your life in misery. Just live. You are lucky that you are alive."

"I wish I were dead. I wish she were alive. I would give my life for her."

"I know, darling. But you can't. Just make her proud. Do something with your life."

She hugged me, and I felt the tears on her cheeks. I didn't know what to say or do to make her feel better. I knew that she had a hole in her heart that couldn't be filled. It is dreadful for parents to bury their children. It should be the other way round. I couldn't imagine how I would feel if I lost a child. I'd been afraid of what she would say to me, but now I felt relieved, although I knew that the guilt would never disappear. No matter what Mary said to me and what my mum told me, I would always feel guilty that Daniela was dead. But she was right about one thing. I was lucky that I was alive, and I had to do something with my life. This was what Daniela would have wanted me to do.

"I will, I promise."

CHAPTER 11

I stayed in the hospital for two more weeks, during which I had enough time to think about my future. My mum and Stephen picked me up from the hospital. She wanted me to come and live with them for a while, because I still needed someone to take care of me. At least, that is what she thought. I was strong and old enough to take care of myself. Besides, I didn't want to bother her. She was seven months pregnant, and she had other things to think about.

Stephen helped me to get to the third floor, because it was quite difficult for me to move on my own with the crutches. Thank God that I used to train every day at the gym. When I stepped through the front door of my apartment, all the memories came flooding back to me. All our conversations, games, dinners, the things we used to do together. I went to the bedroom and opened the wardrobe. I wanted to smell her scent, but there was not a single sign that she had ever existed. All of her clothes were gone.

"Where are her clothes, Mum?"

"I sent them back to her parents."

"Why? Why did you do that without asking me?"

"I thought that it would be better for you if all her things were gone. That it would be easier for you to go on with your life."

"You were wrong! There were things that I wanted to keep. You should've asked me first!"

"Ben, I...I'm sorry. Her mum called and asked for her stuff. I had to do it. I kept the ring, though. It's in the drawer next to your bed."

I opened the drawer and saw the little box on top of my notebook. This was the only thing I had left from her. Then I remembered the picture in my wallet. I wondered if it was still there, or if my mum had thrown it away along with the other stuff that would remind me of her.

"Where's my wallet?"

"Here. I put it in this bag."

"I think I'm fine, Mum. You and Stephen can go now."

"Are you sure, honey? Do you need anything else?"

"No, you can go. Thanks for the help."

"I bought some fruit, veggies, and other things. They're all in the fridge. If you need something, just give me a call."

"OK, Mum, I will."

"And take care for yourself! Your pills are in the drawer, with the instructions. Don't forget to take them. "

"Mum, I'm not a baby anymore. Don't worry about me."

"That's not possible. I'll call you tonight to check if everything is OK."

"Fine."

My mum didn't stop talking about the pills, the food, and the exercises until I'd locked the door behind her. All I wanted was to be on my own and deal with my grief. I lay on my bed, opened the drawer, and took out the little box. Images of what our future together might have been came into my mind. We would've been very happy. I saw myself as a husband. We would've taken a mortgage and bought our own house, where our children would've grown up. We would've grown old together.

But she was gone. All my hopes and dreams had gone with her. I didn't realise that I was crying until I felt the tears. I turned to get my wallet, and then I saw the little rose petal under the wardrobe, probably left by Karisha when she decorated the room. I wondered what had happened to all the candles and decorations. My mum must have cleaned the flat while I was in the hospital, but this one little petal hid under the wardrobe. Even though I couldn't reach it, I was happy to know that it was there. It was as though a part of her was still with me.

I was awakened the next morning by the doorbell. I checked my mobile to see what time it was, and I saw a missed call from my mum. She'd called me the night before, but I didn't hear the phone. Probably she was the one at the door, worried that something had happened to me. I managed to get up and reach my crutches. The doorbell rang again, and I shouted that I was coming.

"Karisha? What are you doing here?"

"I came to see you. Oh, did I wake you up?"

"That's OK. It's midday, anyway. Come in."

Karisha looked pale. Even though it was difficult to tell, I saw a difference in her chocolate skin. I'd never seen her like this, but I wasn't in the best state either. I had no idea why she'd come to see me.

"Sit anywhere you like."

She went into the living room, and I followed her, limping, on the crutches. Karisha sat on the sofa and put something on the table in front of it. When I got close enough, I saw the keys I'd given her before the accident.

"I came to give you back your keys. You look horrible, Ben! Oops, sorry, I didn't mean that."

"It's OK. I know that I look horrible. Maybe a little scary."

"At least you're alive. Again, I didn't mean that. What's wrong with me?"

"Don't worry about it. How are you, Karisha?"

She looked into my eyes and cried. I'd never seen her so sad before. I sat on the sofa next to her and hugged her. Karisha laid her head on my shoulder. I closed my eyes and for a second pretended that it was Daniela sitting next to me, but it wasn't.

"I'm so sorry, Ben...I just...I miss her. I know that I have to be strong and all, but I just can't. I came to you, because you're the only one who can understand how I feel. I'm sorry if I am making you uncomfortable or causing you more pain, but I had to come."

"Hey, Karisha, calm down. It's OK to cry and be sad. I cried all night. I miss her, too. More than you can imagine."

I gave Karisha a tissue, and we talked for more than two hours. She told me stories about her childhood with Daniela, and I have to admit that both of them were very crazy. Karisha laughed and cried as she described to me how she and Daniela used to climb on trees in the park and throw things at people. Their parents had gone completely mad and grounded them for a week.

The two of them had so many memories together. I wished I had spent more time with Daniela. It wasn't enough, and it wasn't fair. I wanted to blame someone for this, to be angry at him and beat him to death. Since the guy who killed her was already dead, I could only blame myself. No matter what Karisha and Daniela's mother told me, I did blame myself.

Karisha and I had lunch together. I wasn't able to cook, so I ordered pizza. I ate so much pizza while I was recovering from the accident that the delivery guy even knew my name. Those pizzas were to die for.

After we finished, Karisha decided to leave because she had a two-hour trip back to Brighton. On her way out, she hugged me. She said that she was happy, because even though her best friend had died, she had another one. I hugged her and told her that she could come or call anytime.

"Karisha, can I ask you for something?"

"Sure."

"Daniela told me that you are a good painter. She told me once that you drew a portrait of her."

"Oh, yeah. I have many. I used to draw a lot when we were in high school. I don't have much time lately. What is it?"

"I...I want to have a tattoo done, but a special one that will remind me of her."

"And you want me to draw it for you?"

"If you can. But if you're busy, don't worry. I'll pick one from the Internet."

"No, no, I will be happy to do it for you. Have you thought of something?"

"No, I haven't. I have no idea what I want. You're the artist, use your imagination. I'm sure that I'm gonna like it."

"OK, Ben. I will let you know when it's ready. I really have to go now. Get better, and take care for yourself."

"Bye, Karisha, and thanks again."

I closed the door behind her, and again I was left all by myself. I realised that with time, my body was going to heal, but Daniela's loss had left a deep wound in my soul that was going to bleed till the end of my days.

CHAPTER 12

It took me a month and a half to recover. I got rid of the crutches and was able to walk on my own again. I felt relieved that I didn't have to use those things anymore. The woman my mum had hired to take care of me when I wasn't able to move without help, left three days before that, and the flat was entirely mine again. I liked her, because she was nice to me, but I didn't feel comfortable having someone else doing my laundry, cleaning, and cooking for me. Besides, I had my own way of doing things, and it was difficult to explain what exactly I wanted done and how to do it.

Karisha called me few times after her visit. She came up with a great idea for the tattoo I wanted, and she returned to my flat to show me the drawing she'd made. When I first saw it, I didn't know what exactly I was looking at, but then I realised that the letter D was in the middle, with angel wings on either side. The wings had three rows of feathers of different sizes and shapes. I'd known that Karisha was good, but the drawing she'd made was so beautiful and tender at the same time. It really did remind me of Daniela, who had been taken away from us too soon. Those wings would've looked great on her beautiful body.

"So...what do you think?"

"It's fabulous. Daniela was right. You are good."

"Thanks. I drew it in one day, but it took me a while to come up with the idea."

"I really like it."

"When are you going to have it done?"

"I'll make an appointment tomorrow."

"So soon?"

"It takes time to get an appointment. I have to make it as soon as possible."

"Have you picked a studio already? I really hope it's not one of those antediluvian ones on the High Road."

"It's not. It's near the Angel station, and it's called Skunx Tattoo. I've heard good things about it."

"I hope you won't regret it later."

"Trust me, I won't."

"I have to go now, Ben. I have lectures. Take care of yourself, and send me a picture of the tattoo once it's done. Oh, I have something else for you."

She took a brown folder out of her bag and gave it to me. When I opened it, I saw a drawing of Daniela. It had been done with charcoal, in different shades and tones of black. When I touched it, my fingers got dirty. For a moment, I stared at it without saying anything. It was a perfect copy of her profile. She held a little daisy in her hand. It looked as if she was almost alive. I moved my forefinger along her cheek and remembered how much I missed her.

"I thought that you would like to have it. I drew it few years ago."

"I don't know what to say...thanks."

"Ben, if you don't want to have it, I'll take it back."

"No, leave it. It's the only thing I have left of her, except the picture in my wallet. My mum took all her stuff away including the framed picture she gave me for Christmas."

"I'm glad that you like it. I have to go now. Talk to you soon."

When Karisha left, I stared at the drawing for a long time, thinking about the great moments I'd had with Daniela. I regretted that I hadn't met her earlier, that I didn't have enough time with her. Sometimes I thought that God was punishing me for something I'd done, or maybe I just didn't deserve to be happy or be loved.

I went to the tattoo studio the next day. It wasn't easy to find. I'd thought it was just behind the station, but I had no idea how wrong I was. Luckily, I had my A–Z map with me. I had to cross the road, walk down Liverpool Road, and take the first street on the left. It took me about ten minutes to get there. The street was full of little shops and places where you could sit and have a cup of coffee in the sun, even though there were not many sunny days in London.

The studio looked like a gallery, but a different kind. There were various types of tattoos everywhere on the walls. It was painted blue, and there was a massive desk a few steps away from the front door. There were catalogues to choose a tattoo from and a leather sofa, where you could sit and wait to be served. I arrived there around noon, and it wasn't busy. I was able to talk with someone straightaway about what I wanted and where I wanted it. He was impressed with the drawing.

"So where do you want it?"

"On my back. How long is it gonna take?"

"Depends. Usually about two to three hours."

"When can I come, then?"

"Let me check." He opened a huge, black appointment book. "You can come on Thursday at 1:00 p.m., if that's OK with you."

"Yes, sure. I'll see you on Thursday, then."

"Have a great day."

On my way home, I thought about my future and what I should do with it. I didn't want to spend the rest of my life as a labourer. Maybe back in the old days it would've been OK for me, but now I wanted something more. I felt like I wanted to help people, to do something for myself. To start a career. Then I remembered what Daniela had told me that last night we'd had together. She told me that I should pursue my dream and become a pilot, but I wanted to start at the bottom, just like my father.

While I waited for my train at Seven Sisters station, my mobile rang. It was my mum. I'd completely forgotten that she wanted me to come over for lunch that day with Stephen. I thought that today was the right time to tell her what I planned to do with my future. I knew that she wouldn't like it, but it was my choice, and she had to accept it. I was old enough to make decisions on my own.

A few minutes later, I stood in front of their door. How was I going to tell her that I planned to spend the rest of my life doing what my father had done, fight for my country? She would never understand.

When I entered the dining room, I saw that the table was already prepared for lunch. My mum had probably ordered food from a restaurant, because she didn't have enough time to cook lately. I felt a bit guilty for forgetting about the visit and not doing anything for her lately. I was feeling selfish again, because the only thing I'd thought about for the last month was Daniela. Mum needed help with all that baby stuff. Stephen was working a lot lately, because they needed the extra money.

"Hey, honey! Wash your hands and get ready for lunch."

"Wow, just like the good old times, Mum."

"But this time you're not shouting at me or running straight to your room," she said, with a smile on her face.

"Hey, Stephen. How are you?"

"I'm good, thanks. Waiting for the little one to come out soon."

"Oh, yeah. Mum, when are you supposed to give birth?"

"End of this month."

"Good, I'll be still here."

"What do you mean? Where are you going, Ben?"

"I've decided to join the army, Mum."

"No! You are not going to do this. You are not going die like your father. I don't want to lose you, too!"

"Mum, calm down. You don't understand. I have to do this. It's what I've always wanted to do, remember?"

"Ben, please don't do this. You have no idea what it is to stay awake all night, to be scared that someone will call you and tell you that your loved one is dead, to live in constant fear. Don't do this to me, please!"

"No, Mum. I've decided already; you can't change my mind. I will do this. I want to do something with my life. Otherwise, I will go crazy."

"So you want me to go crazy, instead. You haven't recovered completely yet."

"But I will have in two months. Mum, please, I really want to do this. I'm not a child anymore; I want to do some good."

"And you think that killing people is good? How are you going to live with the guilt of taking someone's life? You have no idea what it's like."

"Neither do you."

"Yes, I do. I was there when your father used to wake up all sweaty and screaming. You were too young to remember."

"I do remember, and I still want to do it. I don't want to be a builder for the rest of my life."

"You don't have to be, honey. Choose something else. Go to university, but don't go to the battlefield. I don't want to lose you, too, sweetie."

"You won't, I promise."

"Don't make promises you can't keep."

My mum and I kept arguing, while Stephen stood still, without saying anything. I knew that she was scared—terrified, actually—because she knew what it meant to be a soldier. But no matter what she wanted for me and what she thought was best, I wanted to become a soldier like my father. There was nothing left for me here in London, not even in England. My mum had her own family now. I was old enough to take care of myself and to make a decision without asking for permission or help. I knew that I was doing the right thing by joining the army.

CHAPTER 13

It had been a month since I'd got the tattoo on my back. I had to put some kind of ointment on it for the first two weeks. It didn't hurt much while the guy from the studio was doing it. I guess that it was because he used lidocaine while he was working on it. I wasn't able to sleep properly for about a week, but I've had worse wounds than a tattoo.

My mum wasn't happy about it, but she had learned that she shouldn't argue with me. I guess that she was used to all the stupid things I used to do. Maybe I shouldn't have made her nervous or upset, because she was pregnant, but I didn't think about that. She had the baby four days after I had my tattoo done. Stephen called me at 11:00 p.m. on June 8 to tell me that my mum had been escorted to the hospital. I got in the car and drove all the way to Brockley, so that I could be with Mum that day and see the baby.

When I reached the hospital, I asked about my mum at the reception. The woman at the front desk directed me to the second floor. I didn't see Stephen anywhere, so I asked one of the nurses where I could find him. She told me that he was allowed in the room because he was a doctor. I sat on a bench nearby and waited for someone to come out.

My little sister was born at two o'clock in the morning on June 9. They called her Elizabeth. I've always loved that name. She weighed nine pounds and was about twenty-three inches long, quite a big baby. Everybody in my mum's family was tall, including me, so I wasn't surprised. She was in perfect health.

Once the baby was cleaned up, checked by the doctors, and passed through various procedures, Stephen gave her to me. At first I was afraid to touch her or hold her. She looked so small and fragile, but my mum assured me that it was OK. Elizabeth fell asleep in my arms. As I watched her resting in my arms, I thought of Daniela. I'd wanted to have a family with her. I wondered what our children would have looked like. I was never going to find out.

At the end of the month, I went online to check where the nearest armed forces career office was. I could've called or applied online, but I wanted to do everything the old-fashioned way. Besides, I would have the opportunity to see how the soldiers lived and ask all the questions I wanted.

Even though I did my research in June, I decided that it would be better if I applied in September, because I still had to recover from the car accident. So on September 17, I got dressed in a white shirt and black trousers. On the website it said that I could wear whatever I wanted to, but I wanted to look professional and respectful. The office was near the Russell Square tube station on Handle Street, so I took the W3 from the bus stop in front of my flat to Wood Green and then the Piccadilly line to Russell Square.

As I entered the building, my heart jumped. I was shaking, because I didn't know what to expect. I knew only that I was going to have an interview, but not what would happen next. I've always been afraid of the unknown, but I had a good feeling about this. I was doing the right thing by joining the army, and I would never regret it.

One of the sergeants escorted me to an office and asked me to wait there for someone to come and talk to me. The name on the desk read Sergeant M. Griffiths. I wondered if he was the person I was going to talk to. There were a lot of papers on his desk—letters, application forms, maps. I saw a picture of a man in a rugby outfit, who was hugging a boy about ten years old. The man looked familiar, but I couldn't remember where I'd seen him.

I heard someone enter the room. I turned around. It was the same man from the picture, but he wore a uniform. He was tall, like me, and I could tell that he was a sergeant by the three chevrons sewn on his sleeve. My dad had taught me all about the ranks and how to recognize them.

"Good morning!" he said.

"Good morning, sir."

"My name is Sergeant Michael Griffiths, but you can call me Mike, since you are not part of our family yet."

"I'm Benjamin Patrick Johnson, sir. It's nice to meet you."

"Johnson, huh? I knew someone with that surname. He saved my life."

"There are many people with this family name, sir. I guess it's a coincidence."

"Could be. His name was Patrick, Patrick Johnson. He was a pilot. But that was long time ago."

"Sir, it might be a coincidence, but my father's name was Patrick, and he was a pilot, too. He died when I was six."

"What's your mother's name, Ben, if you don't mind me calling you that?"

"No, sir. Her name is Caroline."

"So...you are the Commodore's son. What a surprise."

Sergeant Griffiths told me the story of how my father had saved his life and many more. It was really nice to listen to his stories, because I didn't remember my father much. Griffiths knew him better than I had, which was normal, because he had spent more time with him. For a moment I envied the sergeant and remembered what it felt like to be around my father.

"I'm glad that you came. I've had no contact with your mum and wondered what happened with you two. I can see that you've grown up well, since you want to follow your father's path."

"My mother is not very happy about it."

"I understand her very well. She is afraid that something might happen to you. My mother didn't talk to me for a month after I told her that I want to join the army. But I don't understand one thing, Ben. Why do you want to start at the bottom? You could join the RAF straightaway."

"My grades aren't good enough, and I want to start at the bottom. I want to find out what it's like on the battlefield."

"I see. Well, you should fill in a few application forms and take the BARB test. I'm sure that you know what it is."

"Yes, sir."

"We will have to test your literacy, technological skills, memory, and ability to work with numbers. This isn't going to happen all in one day. I will let you know when you have to come again. Your physical skills will be tested as well. Basically there are a lot of tests before you join us. You will also have to go through a lot of interviews with my colleagues. I will be glad to prepare you for them. You shouldn't be scared or stressed about them, because they are basically going to ask you about yourself and your skills. Do you have any questions?"

"What happens next? I mean after I pass all the tests and interviews?"

"You will be sent to a training camp, where you will be trained how to use different types of guns. You will learn fighting skills. You will be trained to be a soldier, to survive in all kinds of environments. Are you absolutely sure that you want to become a soldier? Because you could start as an officer."

"I am absolutely sure that I want to start my career as a soldier, sir."

"OK, then. This book is for you. It will help you to find out more about a soldier's life. I will call you to let you know when you can come and take the tests. Can you fill this in for me, please?"

"Yes, sir."

It took me about ten minutes to fill in the form Griffiths gave me. We talked for a while about me, my life, and my mother. After we finished with the paperwork, he escorted me to the building exit. On our way out, we met one of the generals, whose name was James Thompson. He was about fifty years old, with grey hair. Griffiths stopped and introduced me to him. When the general found out who my father was, he shook my hand and told me that I should be very proud of him and that everybody would be glad to know that I wanted to follow in his path.

A few days later, Griffiths called me and gave me all the details about the tests. He asked me if I needed help, but I said that I was OK with tests. The part with the interviews was what bothered me. I hated to be questioned, even if it was at a job interview. I didn't like to talk about myself. I have never been the talkative type.

When I arrived at the office on the day Griffiths instructed, I was taken to a large room with many computers. There were a few guys sitting in front of them, waiting for instructions. Some of them were my age, others much older. I sat on an empty chair and waited for the sergeant in front of us to tell me what to do and when.

"Hey, man! Are you nervous?"

"Not really. What about you?"

"I'm shaking, man, seriously. It's like going to an exam."

"Just relax."

"Hey, my name is Derek."

"Ben."

Derek was a twenty-one-year-old Nigerian. He had been born here, and he felt more British than Nigerian, probably because he had been to Nigeria only once. He lived near Cockfosters. His mother was a bank manager, and his father was an estate agent. They wanted him to become a lawyer. He got accepted at Oxford University, studied for two years, and decided that it was not for him. I can imagine how mad his parents must have been when he dropped out of university. He was funny, open-minded, and talkative—all the things I wasn't. We were so different. I don't know why, but I liked him.

The BARB test wasn't difficult. It's only meant to check your ability to understand information and solve problems using your head. There were five sections: reasoning, letter checking, number distance, odd one out—with which I had a lot of fun, especially when Derek laughed the whole time after reading the questions. The sergeant had to warn him to behave or he would be thrown out. The last part was symbol rotation, which was the most difficult for me. At the end of the test, my score was sixty-eight, which meant that I could choose to be a recruit or a geographic technician.

After we'd gone through all the tests, Derek asked me if I wanted to go and grab a pint or two with him. I didn't have any plans for the rest of the day, so we went to the nearest pub along with two other guys, Peter and John. They turned out to be twins, but you would never have guessed, because Peter had black hair and hazel eyes, while John had blonde hair and green eyes.

We talked about who wanted to do what after training camp. Derek joked about becoming an army chef, because he had watched a TV show where army chefs competed against one another. I hadn't even heard of it. The funny thing was that Derek did become a chef, and I have to admit that his food was quite delicious. Peter and John had no idea what kind of position they wanted to take, and neither did I.

I left the pub after the second pint. I was tired, and all I wanted to do was to go home and watch TV. For the first time since Daniela's death, I'd laughed and enjoyed myself. I guess I was just happy that I'd found new friends. People say that the friends you make during your civil service career stay forever, because you have shared an experience that no one else could understand.

CHAPTER 14

Sergeant Griffiths called me on October 6 to inform me that my application was successful. I had to leave for training camp at the end of the month. Since I was a civilian, I had to go through all three phases of training, which meant that I had to spend more than nine months in different schools to develop all the skills I needed to become a soldier.

A few hours later, I received a call from Derek. He was so happy that we were both going to training camp, and of course he already knew that Peter and John were joining us. I really didn't understand how Derek was able to see the bright side of every situation. Well…not until we were on the battlefield. His positive attitude came in handy during many hard times for us.

That same day I went to my mum's house. I had to tell her when I was leaving for training camp. I knew that she wouldn't be as happy as I was. But it was my life, after all, and I didn't want to waste it. There was only one thing that bothered me. I wondered what my father would say if he were alive. Would he support my career choice and be proud of me? Or would he ask me to choose another path? I missed him sometimes. People say that with time, this feeling goes away, but it never does. Every time I'd go to bed and close my eyes, I would see his face, or at least what I remembered of it. He was a great man with a great future. Now that I'd lost Daniela, it was even more difficult for me to fall asleep at night. I thought of both of them, and I wanted to make them proud.

I asked Derek and the boys to help me with moving. I had to move out of the flat in North London. All my clothes, books, everything I had, I left at my mother's house. It wasn't easy, though. I had to say good-bye to all the memories I had of Daniela at this place. Of course I had my childhood memories, too, but they were all filled with pain, regret, and sadness.

"Hey, guys, let's have a party before we all leave for Catterick."

"That's a great idea, mate. My bro and I would love to have some fun before going to that prison."

"It's not a prison. It's a training camp, and we chose it ourselves."

"Why do you always have to be so pessimistic, Ben? I just want to have some fun before we all go to that training camp. God knows what'll happen after that."

"I'm sure that you'll keep your sense of humour and party spirit, Derek."

"Any suggestions?"

"Pete and I know a great strip bar in Windsor."

"That's the spirit, John! Are there any nightclubs there, with beautiful women serving significant amounts of alcohol?"

"Sure. Last time, we went to that place where our cousin works. It was amazing—house music, cheap alcohol, and lovely single women."

"Is that all you can think about?"

"Come on, mate! I'm sure that you've been thinking about it, too."

"I want to have a party, but I'm not interested in women or strip clubs."

"Are you gay?"

"No, Derek, I'm not. I just don't want any distractions."

"Fine, if you say so. Windsor it is, then."

I spent two weeks with my mum, Elizabeth, and Stephen. I couldn't believe how fast my baby sis was growing up. She was able to smile and move her feet and little hands. She made the funny noises that babies do. My mum looked so happy, even though she was tired from changing nappies, feeding her every three hours, and God knows what else.

The day before I left for Windsor, I went to Bruce Castle Park. I felt so lonely since I lost Daniela. I needed to go the place where we were happy, where we spent so many weekends, laughing, playing, and loving each other. I had to be somewhere near her, and since she was buried in another country, I didn't have a place to go to talk to her.

I bought two pink roses from the Turkish shop on the corner and headed to the park. It was about eight o'clock, and the park was almost empty. I wanted to be alone anyway. I didn't want to be around screaming children and boys playing football. I used to love the noise of a ball bouncing on the grass and the screams of the basketball players, but today I had to be alone. I needed some time with her away from all the people.

Daniela loved pink roses. She once said that she wanted a whole garden full of them and a white fence, on which they would grow like ivy on a tree. I laid the roses under the oak tree where we used to have picnics. I had so many things to tell her. I just sat under the tree and started thinking about Daniela.

For a moment I really felt her next to me. I felt her presence, but I knew that this wasn't possible. I stayed at the park for more than two hours. I walked down the lanes and sat on her favourite swing.

It was already dark when I left the park. My mum called me. I told her that I wasn't coming back for dinner. I went to the Goose at Wood Green for a pint and fish and chips with Karisha.

Derek and the twins didn't know that I'd lived in Windsor when I was a kid. I was kind of excited that I was going back there, because I hadn't been to the place for about ten years. My mum used to go there once a month to my father's grave, but I'd never visited that place again, not even for the memorial services she would organise every year with my grandparents. I just wanted to remember him as he was when he was alive. I didn't want to talk to a tombstone or cry over it. But God knows why, on the day we went to that party, I felt that I had to see him and talk to him, even though I knew that he couldn't hear me.

I reached the Windsor station after an hour on the train, which I caught from Ealing Broadway. I noticed how much the place had changed. The old steam train was still there, and of course Windsor Castle was right outside the station, but there were so many new shops, restaurants, and cafés. Luckily, Beaumont Estate was still there. I told the guys about all the ghost stories related to this place, so they insisted that we book a room and stay overnight in the hotel—not that we slept at all.

I checked into the hotel in the afternoon, before my mates arrived. Derek was supposed to share a room with me. Since I was the first one to arrive, I got to choose which bed I wanted. I left my bag there and headed to the centre to buy flowers—red gerberas, Dad's favourite. It wasn't easy to find them though. Most of the flower shops had roses mainly, or if they had gerberas, they were pink, Daniela's favourite colour.

It wasn't easy to find the place where he was buried. I couldn't remember where exactly his grave was, and the cemetery had changed so much since the last time I'd visited it. As I walked down the alleys in search of my father's resting place, I saw a blonde girl who was kneeling on someone's grave. She kissed the tombstone, left the roses she was holding, and headed to the alley where I was walking. I know that it sounds strange, but at that moment I felt as if I knew this girl, although I had no idea where I'd seen her before. She passed by me, looked right into my face, and smiled. I stopped for a moment and turned around to look at her, but she didn't stop, and she walked through the gate of the cemetery.

After twenty meters I saw the black tombstone my mum had ordered. I would have recognized it anywhere. Even though it had ivy grown all over the back of it, I knew that it was my father's. It looked deserted, and no wonder, since no one took care of it. My mum was too busy with her new life, and my grandparents lived too far to come.

And here I was, kneeling in front of my father's grave, not knowing what to say or do. I left the flowers at the foot of the tombstone and stood up. For a moment I felt guilty in a way for leaving him, for not coming more often, and for not talking to him. But he was dead. How can you talk with a dead person? He was gone, just like Daniela. I wondered how he would feel if he knew the things I'd done, the people I'd hurt. One thing I knew for sure was that he would have loved Daniela, because she was the only good thing that had ever happened to me. Unfortunately, God had other plans for her. It's funny how people fall in love so easily. I knew I was never going to love another woman in my life, even if that meant that I would die alone. I was never going to betray her or forget her.

I left the cemetery with thoughts of my father and Daniela. I wondered if they were somewhere else, in another dimension or place, watching me. But I'd never believed in other lives. I didn't believe in that afterlife bollocks.

CHAPTER 15

I picked up the boys from the train station at seven o'clock that evening. They were ready for the strip club, but I didn't want to join them on that little adventure. Derek left his sack in our room. After he'd asked me a hundred times if I'd change my mind, he left with the twins. They planned to go to a pub first to get decently drunk and then make their way to the strip club. I, on the other hand, had other plans. The only thing I wanted at that moment was to go to the swimming pool for an hour or two, take a relaxing bath, and watch TV.

I must have fallen asleep while I was watching *CSI Miami*. My phone rang and woke me up. It was Pete, who told me that they were already at the nightclub. He asked me if I was going to join them.

"Hey, sleeping beauty, are you coming or not?"

"What? Oh, yeah, sure. I'll see you there, mate."

Before I received the call from Pete, I'd had a strange dream. Daniela was there. She was standing on a path somewhere in a huge park, and when I tried to get near her, she smiled at me and ran away. I chased her, but I was just a child, about five or six years old, and I couldn't catch her. She went farther and farther away from me. I kept running, but I stumbled and fell on the ground. When I got up, Daniela was gone. There was blood coming from my left knee, and my elbows were scratched. I sat on the path and cried. All of a sudden I felt a hand on my shoulder. I turned around and saw a little girl. Her blonde hair was tied back, but I wasn't able to see her face, because the sun was shining right in my eyes. She asked me if I was all right and said that she could help me. I wanted to know her name and why she was there, but then the phone rang.

I woke up in a sweat. It must have been the dream that caused it or the hot bath I'd taken before I went to bed. I took a shower before I left the hotel to meet my mates. I wasn't even in the mood for a party. I only wanted to stay in my room, but I couldn't just leave them alone. They were my mates. Besides, they would never understand, and I had no intention of sharing anything about Daniela with them. I put on my black jeans and a white T-shirt and went to the reception to call a cab.

While I waited outside, I lighted a fag and kept thinking about Daniela. Even though it had been six months since her death, I felt as though it wasn't right to have fun, enjoy life, and move on with my own life. Maybe this was one of the main reasons I had signed up for the army. Somewhere deep inside my heart, I prayed to die, so I could be with her again. I didn't think about my mum and how she would feel; I only thought about my pain, my wish, and my guilt.

Derek and the other two were sitting at a table near the bar. I wondered how they'd managed to get a table on a Friday night, especially in this bar. I'd heard that it was the best and most expensive one in Windsor. But to be fair, all bars looked the same to me—full of drunken women in short skirts, dancing provocatively, waiting for someone to notice them and buy them more drinks. The furniture was all black and white, which was logical since the club's name was the Black and White. The bartenders were dressed in suits, and the waitresses looked as if they came from the housekeeping department of a public house in France. There were golden disco balls on the ceiling. I really don't understand some people's taste or these posh designers' ideas.

I had to wait for about twenty minutes just to get a single JD and Coke. The bar was packed, mainly with women who were trying to get to the handsome bartenders. Once I got my drink, I sat at the table next to Derek. He was already drunk, just like the twins, and couldn't wait to tell me all about the girls in the strip club.

"Let me tell you about Denise. Oh, she was gorgeous. Her boobs were like watermelons. She was dressed in a pink skirt with feathers, and when she danced for me..."

"OK, I think I've heard enough."

"No, no, no...You didn't come, so you have to hear all about it. Seriously, man, we're going to soldier training camp; you probably won't see a woman for the next six months."

"What about the women there?"

"I mean real women, Pete. Not man-looking, full-of-muscles types."

"I didn't know that you were gay, Ben. I learn new things about you every day."

"I'm not gay, Derek! I just don't want to waste my time on women with a questionable reputation."

"Too bad, because that blonde over there is checking you out."

"That's just your imagination, Derek."

"No, it's not. Look, she's doing it again. At the table next to the pillow, with the green dress."

I wasn't interested, but when I looked at her, I realised that it was the girl I'd seen at the cemetery. It was dark, but I was sure that it was her. What a strange coincidence! And Derek was right; she was looking at me. I had no idea why, but it was probably because she recognized me as well. She caught me looking at her and smiled at me.

"She's smiling at you, lover boy."

"Enough, Derek! Let's just enjoy ourselves."

"Oh, no, I won't leave it like this. Wait here."

"Derek, what the..."

"You'll thank me later."

He didn't hear me calling him to come back. Pete and John laughed, because they knew what was coming. Derek was always like this—wayward. He loved to put his nose where it didn't belong, and that didn't always end well. He would start fights, flirt with the wrong girls, and mess up everything. But I have to admit, that guy knew how to live without fear or restraint. You might think that he was a bad person, but I have to say that he was always trying to help. Even though I'd never told him, he knew that there was something wrong with me, something that I didn't want to share with anyone. He tried to make me feel happy, laugh, enjoy myself. At the end, he turned out to be my best friend.

After about ten minutes, Derek came back to the table, laughing. I knew that he was up to no good. God knows what he'd told that girl. I was sure that he'd tried to convince her that I wanted a date or her phone number.

"You won't believe this. She knows you."

"Yes, she saw me earlier today."

"I'm not talking about that. She said that she knows you from before. She wasn't sure at first, but when I told her your name, she said that she knows you for sure."

"How come?"

"I have no idea, bro. She didn't tell me. She said that she wants to talk to you."

"I'm not going over there."

"No need, she's coming to us."

The girl wore a green dress, with short sleeves, that was a little bit above her knees. She was about five feet tall, but the shoes she wore made her look taller. Her hair was tied in a bun, except for her fringe, which covered half of her face. I have to admit that this girl was very beautiful, slim, and well built. The twins' eyes were all over her, and I saw many guys turn their heads to watch her as she approached our table.

She sat next to me and shouted in my ear, because the music was too loud to hear her. "Are you Benjamin Johnson?"

"I...yes, I am. Do I know you?"

"You don't remember me?"

"Ah...no, I'm sorry, but I don't."

"Oh, don't worry. That's normal. You were just six when you left the house. We've both changed a lot."

"I'm sorry. Who are you?"

"I'm Emma. You used to live in the house next door. We played every weekend in the park."

Sure, I remembered her. She was one of the kids I'd grown up with. Her parents used to take us for picnics every weekend. Her father would fix things in our house when my dad was away. We played in the back garden for hours. She wouldn't want to leave, because my mum made the best sandwiches in the world. Emma was quite a round girl when we were kids. No wonder I didn't recognize her. She'd turned from an ugly duckling into a beautiful swan.

"You've changed a lot."

"I'm not the only one. How's your mum doing?"

"She fine, probably tired from all the nappy changing and sleepless nights."

"You have a baby?"

"No, she has a baby. She got married again."

"I have to go back to the girls, but can we have tea tomorrow?"

"Sure, why not?"

"OK, noon at Costa. The one by the station."

"I'll be there."

Emma went back to her table, and we spent the rest of the night drinking. Derek kept reminding me that I had him to thank for helping me get a date. I kept saying that this was not a date, just a reunion of old friends. He didn't seem to believe me, but I didn't care. I'd only agreed to see her because she used to be a good friend of mine, part of a life I had forgotten.

I woke up at nine o'clock the next morning, and the first thing I saw was Derek lying on his bed like a dead person. When I heard his snoring, I knew that he wouldn't wake up until at least one o'clock. I took a shower and went to the restaurant to have breakfast. The smell of bacon reminded me of when I was a child and my mum cooked almost every morning. Emma would come for breakfast sometimes. Her parents didn't want to let her come so early, but my mum didn't mind. She was lonely without my father. She wanted more people around her, even if it meant that she had to deal with two crazy children, full of energy.

I arrived at Costa early and decided to smoke a fag while I was waiting for Emma to come. I'd stopped smoking for Daniela, but after her death, I'd started again. Even though I knew that it wasn't good for my health, after the accident I didn't care. Cigarettes were the only thing that made me feel good after I lost her.

"That's a bad habit."

"I've heard that before."

She ordered English breakfast tea with milk and a chocolate muffin. Emma had always loved chocolate. I remember how she used to come and eat half of my mother's muffins. Her excuse was that her own mum couldn't cook, and she was not allowed to eat chocolate at home.

"I see that you still love chocolate muffins."

"And that's the only thing that hasn't changed about me."

"I've noticed."

Emma was two years older than me. She'd graduated in film production at Thames Valley University and found a job at Ealing Studios, which was exactly what she wanted, or at least that's what she told me. Her parents had moved out, but she'd stayed in their old house with one of her colleagues from the university.

I didn't share much with her. I was more interested in what she had been doing during the past few years. Every time she asked me something about my personal life, I changed the subject, but I did give her the address of the training camp. I told her that it would be easier if she called me, but she wanted to correspond with me in the old-fashioned way, by post.

We talked about our old friends from the street. I'd wondered what all of them had been doing since I'd left the place. She told me that old Mrs Martin still went out every afternoon at four o'clock, wearing a different hat every day, to feed the pigeons in the park. When I was a child, I couldn't understand why she did it. I'd laughed at her, because she had pigeons on her hat. Emma told me that she had lost her husband in World War II, and she had never got married again. She didn't have children, and I never saw anyone talking to her. Mrs Martin must have been one very lonely woman.

After three hours of talking and laughing, we left the coffee shop. I asked Emma if she wanted me to take her home, but she said that she had another appointment. She hugged me and headed to the park.

On my way back to the hotel, I couldn't stop thinking about Mrs Martin. Was that my future? Standing in a park all alone, feeding the pigeons? I was never going to fall in love again. I didn't want to be with another woman.

CHAPTER 16

"Are you sure that you want to do this?"
"Yes, Mum, I am sure."
"You can still resign."
"No, I made a decision, and I'll stick to it."
"You are so pigheaded."
"I don't want to argue, Mum. Face it, I'm going to training camp, and after a year, I'll go to the battlefield...Afghanistan, Iraq...anywhere. And you have to accept it. I'm not a child anymore."

My mum looked at me with such sorrow in her heart. I understood why she was worried. She didn't want to lose me the way she'd lost my dad, but I was old enough to make my own decisions, to take care of myself.

"Mum, I'll be fine, I promise."
"Don't make promises you can't keep."
"Good luck, Ben!"
"Thanks, Stephen. Take care of my mum and my little sister."
"I will. You take care for yourself, boy. And don't forget that you are always welcome in our house."

I hugged my mum, said good-bye to both of them, and kissed my baby sis on her cheek. I watched the car leave and wondered how my mum must be feeling. I picked up my sack and headed to the entrance.

Derek was already in our room, waiting for me. He had arrived a few days earlier, and he had already rearranged the place. There were pictures of lingerie models all over one of the walls. He had a blue carpet with the Chelsea logo on it, which didn't go with anything in the room except the signed poster of Lampart and the Chelsea sheets. The twins didn't have anything against the decorations Derek had, because they were Chelsea fans, too. I can't say the same for the sergeant, who asked him to remove all the teenage stuff from the room, because we were not there to have fun.

It wasn't exactly what I expected a room at training camp to be like. My bed was opposite Derek's, and I have to admit that it was very comfortable. But it didn't help me with my insomnia. Every night, after a whole day of running, training, and studying, I would lie on my bed, listening to Derek snore, and think about my future, my family, and most of all, Daniela. No matter how many months, days, and hours had passed since I'd lost her, I just couldn't forget her.

The first phase of training lasted about fourteen weeks. I learned a lot of new skills, but it wasn't easy. I had problems with the rifle. I just couldn't get used to it, especially the rebound after shooting. I had bruises all over my left shoulder. I had to work harder than most of the guys to learn how to shoot properly. Every morning I would wake up at four o'clock and run for five miles. Because of the accident, I had pain in my knees and my left elbow when I was physically loaded. The pain made it almost impossible for me to climb walls, run fast, or throw grenades at the targets. I didn't want to show my weakness to the rest of the guys at the camp or to the sergeants who were training us. After I was done with my five miles, I would go to the training ground and complete all the exercises at least once. By the time Derek and the twins were awake, I was already in the shower, ready for another day of what they called torture. I spent more time in the library preparing myself for the courses than anyone else. Not because I wanted to be the best, or first, but because for the first time in my life, I felt that this was the right place for me. And even though I was away from my relatives, I felt as if I were home.

Life at training camp was not what I expected. I'd thought that we would live in isolation, that we wouldn't have time for anything except training and books, but I was wrong. That place was massive. There were more than fourteen barracks and training grounds that reproduced different types of atmospheres and conditions that we would one day face. To me, the place looked like a huge paintball playground, similar to the one at Effingham where I'd go with my colleagues from work. We played pool on the weekend, had fun, and went out and enjoyed ourselves. Most of the guys spent all their money on games and nightclubs. I preferred to keep my salary in the bank, because I wanted to have my own place to live when I retired or decided to do something else. I spent money only when I was visiting my mum, but I visited her only twice during my training. Derek and the twins, on the other hand, went back to their families every weekend.

Some of the soldiers at the camp complained about the food, the training, the attitude of the sergeants, and the rooms we lived in. Derek made jokes about everything. He was an optimist, and I doubted that anyone or anything would change his attitude towards life. If it wasn't for him, I would've lived in complete isolation during those fourteen weeks. He introduced me to most of the people who lived at Catterick. But I wasn't interested in having conversations with people I'd just met. I preferred to spend my time at the training ground, rather than listen to people cry about how much they missed their friends and families. I knew that being a soldier meant working as a team, but I thought that if I was prepared for every situation, if I was trained and physically prepared, I had a better chance of saving more people.

With time, I became someone with no personal feelings. Nothing could make me feel happy or smile with all my heart. Not even the photos of my little sister, not the letters from Karisha or Emma. Derek noticed that something was wrong with me because I stopped going out for drinks with the twins and him. I closed myself off completely from the rest of the world. The only thing I cared about was the training ground.

After eight months at Catterick and a few other places where I was sent during the process, I finished my soldier training successfully. What made me proud was that I was the best. I was ready for what was coming next. I knew that I was about to leave my country and defend it, but I wasn't afraid that I might never come back.

Since I didn't have my own place, I had to spend two months with my mum and Stephen. He offered to pick me up from Catterick, but I wanted to travel by train with my friends.

Stephen had a spare room in his house especially for me, where I had put all my clothes and stuff after I'd left the flat. When I entered my room, I saw all the boxes, still packed, with yellow labels on them saying what was inside. It was just the way I'd left it eight months ago. During the few times I visited my mum while I was at training camp, I didn't have enough time, or maybe I didn't want to. I opened the box that said "Memories" and took the little jewellery box out of it, along with the aeroplane my father bought for me at the Royal Air Force Museum. I lay on my bed and thought of her. She was so beautiful and fragile. It was been more than a year since she'd been gone, and I had so much to tell her. She used to say that every time she was sad or missed someone, she would write the person a letter or record it in her diary. It was about two o'clock in the morning. I took a piece of paper and a pen, which had "Middlesex Hospital" engraved on it, and wrote her a letter.

Dear Daniela,

I was never good at writing letters, but I have so many things to tell you, and this is the only way I can do it. I miss you so much. I wish you were here to see everything that has been happening in my life lately. My mum gave birth to a girl, Lizzie. My baby sis looks a lot like my mum, but she has Stephen's eyes. He's been very generous with me. I didn't expect him to accept me, but he treats me like his own son. I've just finished my soldier training. Remember that night when you told me that you thought that I should do something with my life? Well, I have. I decided to follow my father's path and become a pilot. But I wanted to start at the bottom. I'm still waiting for Sergeant Griffiths to inform me where I'm going. I hope that I will be deployed to Afghanistan. There are so many soldiers dying there. I wish I could help them. I know that if you were here, you would be terrified, but I'm not scared. I want be brave, just like you. You went out on a date with a complete stranger and then moved in with him. I love you so much, my angel. I wish I could spend more time with you, hear your voice again, and hold you my arms. You are the love of my life, and I think of you every single minute. You have no idea what pain I felt when you left me. I'm sure that you already knew that I was about to propose to you that night when I lost you, but I didn't have the chance. You are gone now, not only because of him, but because of me. I couldn't make you stay, even though I couldn't live without you. You are the first woman I've loved, and the only one I will ever feel so close to. I still remember the scent of your skin, the taste of your lips, and the beat of your heart when you were lying next to me. I'm holding the ring I bought for you. I can't figure out why this happened to us. Why you had to leave me all alone, why destiny and God wanted us to be apart. I had so many plans for the wedding, for our life together. I never told you, but I wanted to buy my old house in Windsor so we could spend the rest of our lives together, in the place where I'd lived with my father, and play in the back garden with our children just like I used to play with him. But that's not possible, because you are gone. I would give everything to see you again, even for a second. You will always be in my heart, Daniela. No matter where you are now, you are my angel, my first and only love, my saviour, my destiny.

Love, Ben

I put the pen down and folded the letter. I found an envelope in one of the desk drawers and put the letter inside. Daniela was right; I felt relieved, just as when I used to talk to her in the park under our oak tree. I switched on the telly, because I was having trouble sleeping, and searched through the channels until I found *Boomerang*. I remembered the time when Daniela and I watched *Tom and Jerry*. She laughed every time Jerry hit Tom with a bat or a pipe. She said that she'd always wanted to have a cat, but she wasn't allowed, because her mother was allergic. She wanted to call it either Tom or

Crookshanks, because she was a big *Harry Potter* fan. Unfortunately, she never got to read the last book. I'd bought it for her when it came out, but she never had time to read it and find out how the story ended. After she died, I couldn't even keep the books, because my mum sent all her stuff back to her parents.

I had no idea when I fell asleep that night, but I woke up at eight o'clock. My mum had to leave for work, so she woke me up, because I was her babysitter for the next two months. I didn't mind spending time with my little sister, because she was so sweet. Every time she smiled at me, all the tension in my shoulders eased. It wasn't easy to take care of a baby, but I managed to feed her, change her nappies, and put her to sleep. I would take her to one of the parks. Sometimes Derek kept me company, but he wasn't good at taking care of babies. He was good at being a complete idiot or looking like a clown in front of them. But it didn't surprise me, because he was a grown-up baby himself.

Three weeks after I went back to my mum's place, I received a letter. My mother saw it first and gave it to me with tears in her eyes.

"It's for you."

"What is it?"

"A letter from the British Army."

I opened the letter and read it. My mum stood next to me. Her face was pale and full of grief. She knew what the letter was about.

"Where are they sending you?"

"Afghanistan."

She didn't say a word after she heard my answer. She ran to her room and closed the door. I heard her crying, but I didn't know what to say or do to make her feel better. I wasn't going to change my mind, and she knew it. I had to leave for Afghanistan in six weeks.

CHAPTER 17

I left for Camp Bastion a few weeks after I received the letter. We took off from Brize Norton in Oxfordshire. When I arrived at the airport, I felt as though I was going on a really long holiday, from which I might never return. All the soldiers had to check in, as if they were going on a civilian flight. The only difference was that the aeroplane we flew on was not a Boeing or an Airbus but a Royal Air Force TriStar.

Once the plane took off, I looked out of the window and thought about my family and the moments I'd spent with them. I watched the green fields of England become smaller and smaller, until all the sheep and horses wandering around them disappeared. I wondered if I was going to see this beautiful land, feel the rain on my shoulders, or smell the aroma of freshly cut grass again.

The journey to Kandahar took about seven hours. Luckily, I had my mates to have fun with. Derek was making a complete clown of himself in front of all the soldiers. He was so happy to meet new people, because there were guys who'd come from other camps, and soldiers who had already been there once or twice. We listened to their stories, and I thought that they were exaggerating. Then I saw the situation there with my own eyes.

We travelled during the night. When everybody fell asleep, I had time to read one of the books I'd brought along with me. It was Daniela's favourite book—*Nights at Rodanthe*—after Harry Potter, of course. I was happy that my mum had forgotten to give some of her books back to her parents. I was able to feel what she must have felt when she read this book. I remember when she bought it. Even though there was a movie based on the book, and she'd already seen it, she said that she wanted to read it anyway, because books represented the whole story better than movies. I smiled at her, because I had no idea what she meant by that. I watched movies all the time, and I loved them, but I never had the time or the will to read a book.

A few hours later, one of the sergeants woke everybody and told us to put on our uniforms, body armour, and helmets, because we were already in Afghanistan. I would never forget the first time I stepped onto this land. Even though it was late at night, I could feel the humidity. There was a strong wind blowing, and I was able to see the sand dancing around the searchlight. We had to board another plane to get to Camp Bastion, which was the main operating base.

Some of the soldiers were sent to other camps. The twins left one week after we arrived, with another group. Derek was very disappointed. Our little gig was broken up, and it was just two of us left on our own. He promised to take care of me, but I didn't need any protection. I was stronger than he was and more focused. He was absentminded sometimes. I knew that I would have to keep him safe. He was a great fighter, though, and there was no doubt that if he got into a fight, he would win. But I was more observant.

After two months we were moved to a base in the southwest part of the country, near Lashkar Gah, the capital of Helmand province, which was not that far from the main base. It wasn't as big as Bastion where we had all the facilities we needed, including a huge medical centre. The wounded troops were transported to the main base before they were taken back to the United Kingdom or the United States. There were about six thousand soldiers there, which was less than a third as many as at the main base. Some of them would come for a few days and then leave, while others were there for more than a year. I met many US soldiers there, and Derek was more than happy to talk with them.

Sometimes I felt it wasn't that bad to be there—to protect my country, learn how to survive, save other people's lives. We used to gather around, when we were not patrolling, and talk about our families. I learned so much about the guys I worked with. Some of them were even younger than me, and others already had four kids back at home. They would show pictures of their children, their wives, husbands, parents. All of them had a talisman, which they always kept with them. I wondered how their loved ones slept at night. How did a woman with four kids go to bed, thinking about her husband and wondering if she would ever see him again? And all these female soldiers—how did their fathers feel every time they heard the phone ring? How they must miss their children. I remember how my mum used to cry at night when she thought I was asleep, and the relief on her face when she hugged my father every time he came back. I knew that she must be doing the same thing now because of me, and I hated myself for doing this to her. Even though Derek had promised her that he would bring me back alive, she must have thought about the possibility that she might never see me again. I had to spend two years here without going home.

But I wasn't worried. I had my talisman with me too, and I was sure that she would protect me. Daniela's picture was always there, near my heart. Even though I wanted to join her in death, even though I missed her so much that it hurt, I knew that I had to stay alive for my mum and my little Lizzie. I wanted her to know me, to remember me. I wanted to be part of her life.

My mum sent me letters twice a month with pictures of Lizzie. She said that my sister was trying to talk already, but it was difficult to understand what she was saying. Lizzie took her first steps during their holiday in Valencia. My mum loved Spain. She wanted to visit every single place there. I was more interested in Australia, Canada, the United States...the places where people spoke English. I was happy to hear new things from the family, especially now that the little devil was growing so fast. My mum complained a few times that once Lizzie started walking, she began to break things. She opened the fridge all by herself to play with the eggs. I could only imagine the mess, but every time I'd read one of Mum's letters, I just couldn't stop laughing. My sister was one little troublemaker, just like me.

Mum was not the only person who sent me letters. Karisha also wrote to me once or twice a month. There was not much to say though. She was in her final year of university, and I quote, "life is as boring as it has always been." Derek saw me reading a letter from her one day and asked me who this chick was. I had no secrets from him, except for Daniela. She was the only thing I didn't want to talk about. He was more curious than a five-year-old child, but I never told him about Daniela or what my tattoo meant.

"So, are you going to tell me who that chick is?"

"You know, you should've become a journalist or a police officer."

"I can use those skills when we catch someone and torture him."

"You are already torturing me. Why on earth did I agree to live under the same roof with you?"

"Because we are besties. Now tell me about the girl."

I showed him a picture of Karisha and told him that I once knew her sister. From the look on his face, I figured that he must have liked what he saw very much. Also, he asked me for her address.

"I'll have to ask her first. I can't just give it to you."

"I'm not a stalker, Ben."

"I know, but I can't give it to you."

"Hey, Ochinyabo, Johnson! Stop arguing like teenage girls, and get ready. We have a mission."

"Yes, sir!"

Derek and I put on our body armour and helmets, took our weapons, and jumped on the truck. Sergeant Thomas explained what we had to do. It was a routine check of one of the villages. I hated these missions. Not because I was afraid or bored, but because I wanted to cry every time I saw how the local people lived. Most of their houses were blasted, but there were children playing around them. There were huge holes from bullets and spots of blood on the walls. Some of the villages we visited had no clean water or food. I saw many women with babies in their arms and kids running around them, but instead of being happy and enjoying life, they were forced to live in misery. I couldn't watch them. I wondered why all of this had happened. Innocent people were suffering because someone's sick idea of justice was to kill three thousand people by blowing up a building or a tube station. It wasn't fair. But I'd signed on for it, and I had to finish what I'd started. These moments made me realise how insignificant my own pain was.

When we arrived at the village, it was unusually quiet. It looked as if it had been deserted for some time. We couldn't see anyone or anything moving. The signal we'd received at base was about a few rebels who were part of a terrorist organisation. Sergeant Thomas told us that they were planning to hit the base, so we had to hit them first.

The sergeant asked us to split into three groups and search the place. Derek, John, Roger, Harry, and I turned left and walked down a deserted street. I knew all of them very well. John had a big family: three kids, a wife, and four sisters. He was the only son his parents had. His youngest daughter, who was only five years old, had given him a small, plush pink pig, called Piglet. He used to carry it everywhere with him. Harry was younger than me, but very mature. Roger was the head of the team and the oldest. He ordered us to go inside a building that looked like a temple and search it. When we entered the place, I heard a noise, but I thought that it was only my imagination. I asked everyone to stay still, and I heard it again. There was something moving in there—or someone.

All of a sudden a grenade fell on the ground, and everything went blurry. Roger shouted at us to hide somewhere and wait for the others to come. Derek and I hid behind one of the walls.

"Bloody hell! What was that?" asked Derek.

"Definitely not a genie, mate."

"Too bad. I've always wanted to see one."

We couldn't see the other three and hoped that they were OK. I could only hear gunshots and screams. I prayed that my mates were alive and well.

I couldn't just stay in one place and hide. Derek begged me to stay with him and think about myself, but I had to know what had happened to the other three. When I ran into the open space, Derek followed me. I heard him say, "You stupid wayward idiot!" as he ran after me. We walked side by side until I saw a man coming towards us. He pointed a shotgun at me, and I shot him. Another man attacked us, but Roger came out of nowhere and took him down.

The place went silent again. I couldn't hear anyone moving except the three of us. We waited for the dust to settle, and Roger called for John and Harry.

"Right here!" I heard John scream.

We followed his voice. As we walked down the corridor of the temple, I counted six bodies. John walked towards us with Harry, both of them relieved that they'd survived the shooting. I stopped for a moment. I'd never seen a corpse before, and the sight of so many dead bodies made me feel sick. They were all riddled with bullets. I saw blood everywhere. The man I'd killed was lying there motionless. I felt guilty for a moment, because this man might have a family, people who loved him, but being a soldier meant that taking someone else's life was part of the job description.

I stood behind my colleagues and looked at the man's face. I knew that I would never forget it. I had no idea how I would deal with my guilt. Just then, one of the men, who we'd thought was dead, raised his hand and pointed his weapon at my fellow soldiers. Roger saw him, but he couldn't react, because John stood in front of him. Before I could do anything, the man shot John, and he fell on the ground. Roger shouted at us to hide and killed the man who had shot at us.

The rest of the squad heard the shooting, but by the time they arrived, it was too late. The rest of the guys walked around the place to check that it was empty and that all the men were dead. While they did that, I knelt next to John and took his hand.

"You'll be fine. Just hang on."

"Johnson, please..."

"Don't talk. You are losing a lot of blood."

"Please...give this back to my daughter."

"You will be fine, Watson. Hang on. You'll give it to her yourself."

"Tell my wife I love her."

"No, Watson! Watson, wake up! Wake up, mate! You'll be fine."

But he wasn't. By the time we reached the base, John had died. He died in my arms, holding his daughter's piglet. Another person had died because of me, because I wasn't cautious enough, because I was too busy with my own thoughts. I had no idea how I would go to his family and face his wife and his children. He was a great man, just like my father. John had two weeks left in Afghanistan. He had to be back for Amy's birthday. If I'd seen that man earlier, if I had shot him first, John would be alive. But I hadn't.

When we returned to the base, Roger and Sergeant Thomas reported to the lieutenant what had happened during the mission. I was tired and went back to my tent. Unfortunately, I wasn't left alone.

One of the corporals came in. "Johnson, you have mail."

"Cheers."

I wasn't in the mood for reading. But then I saw that the letter was from Emma. She wrote to me almost every month. At first our letters were all about past events, people we knew, her family, gossip. After a while she started sharing personal things with me, asking for advice or complaining about her work. In the two years I spent in Afghanistan, we became very close. I cared about her in a strange way. Derek would joke about her a lot. He said that once I got back to London, I had to take her on a date. Maybe he was right. She was one attractive young woman, and even though

I never asked her, she told me that she had no boyfriend and no intention of looking for one after the last one she'd had. Emma told me all about him in her letters. They'd met at university, and he asked her out after three months. She was happy with him until she found out that he was cheating on her. When she broke up with the guy, he started stalking her. She said that it wasn't easy to get rid of him. She was still afraid that he might do something to her.

I opened the envelope and smelled the aroma of her perfume. The letter was written on a piece of pink paper from the notebook her mum had bought her after she graduated. She would always send me letters written in this notebook with a black pen. When I read the first few sentences, I was stunned.

Dear Ben,

Let's skip the part where I ask you how you are doing, I know that it must be very hard for you to be away from your family and blah blah. I'm sorry for my language. I just have something amazing to tell you and can't wait. Your old house in Windsor is for sale! Can you imagine? I was shocked, too. Mrs Lewis said that she wants to move out with her husband, because the house is too big for them. You know what this means, don't you? You can have your house back, and we can be neighbours again. I know that this is exactly what you want. I spoke with her, and she said that she would be more than happy to meet you, if you are still interested. If you need any help with the mortgage or need a loan, count on me. I know that you would never ask me for money, but I had to say it. Anyway, I really hope that you are alive and well, and I can't wait to see you once you get back. Don't forget that you promised to take me to London to see your little sister and your mum. By the way, how is Derek doing? I hope that he's not being a pain in the ass as always. Send my regards to him.

PS—I still remember what you said about that place you wanted to visit once you come back. May I come with you? I don't know why it is so important to you, and I'm not going to ask, but I would love to see that oak tree.

Emma

CHAPTER 18

I wasn't able to go to John's funeral, because I still had three months left in Afghanistan. I didn't want to go, anyway. I knew that it was a matter of respect, but I knew what these funerals were like. I just couldn't stand there and pay my respects to his family, knowing that I could've saved him.

In two years I'd lost many fellow soldiers, but most of them I didn't know very well. John was the only one I'd felt close to. I admired him. He was strong and determined, and unlike many people, he had a happy family, a woman who loved him, and children who adored him. He was their hero, as my father was mine.

I had no idea how I would face his family and talk about him. I've been in their place. I knew how difficult it must have been for his wife to explain to their children that they wouldn't see their father again. I wondered if they would remember him when they grew up, or if the memory of him would just fade away with time. I barely remembered my father. I remembered how he looked, but I'd forgotten his voice, his smile, my childhood with him. Even though my mum did her best to keep the memory of him alive, I closed myself off from it, because it was easier that way.

Two days after I was back in London, I bought a ticket to Southend-on-Sea. I didn't want to postpone my meeting with John's family, but that didn't make me less afraid of going.

John's family lived in a house on Earl's Hall Avenue. It wasn't easy to find the street, but luckily the locals were very polite and helpful. I asked an old couple how to find the house, and they gave me directions.

It took me about fifteen minutes to find the place. It was noon on Saturday, and I knew that his family would be home. I hadn't called to inform John's wife that I was coming, because I had no idea what to say. To be honest, I didn't even know how to start the conversation.

The house was quite big, bigger than the one we'd had in Windsor. I saw a silver car parked in front of it. A blonde woman was taking a lot of orange bags from Sainsbury's out of the trunk.

"Excuse me, do you know if this is Joan Watson's house?"

"Yes, I'm Joan. How can I help you?"

"My name is Benjamin Johnson. I served with your husband."

I saw the sadness in her eyes. She looked tired, and she had shadows under her blue eyes. I knew exactly how she felt. She must have cried every single night when the children were asleep. Joan reminded me of my mum. I felt sorry for this woman, and at the same time I admired her courage, because she didn't give up.

She put the bags on the ground and locked the car, then pointed to the house and asked me to go in. I took half of the bags and followed her.

When I entered the house, the first thing I saw was a picture of the whole family. It was taken on the beach. They stood in front of a sand castle. They looked so happy.

"Would you like something to drink Mr Johnson?"

"Just a glass of water, please."

While she was in the kitchen, I sat on a black sofa and looked at all the photos of John and his family. There were drawings by his children hanging on the walls. One of them was by Amy. It showed John in a uniform, with the word DADDY under it. During his stay in Afghanistan, I'd seen many of these drawings. His wife used to send them along with her letters.

"So what is it that you wanted to talk about, Mr Johnson?"

"You can call me Ben. I...I don't know where to start, Mrs Watson."

"Please, call me Joan."

"John used to talk a lot about you. I feel like I already know you. He was a great man, and I'm sorry for your loss. I'm sure you've heard that already, but I know how you feel. I lost my father when I was six, the same way you've lost your husband."

"I know, John told me. He used to talk about all his colleagues in his letters. I've seen some of them in the pictures he would send me."

"I'm not here to soothe you, because I know that no one and nothing can do that. I'm just fulfilling my duty. I promised John that I would return this to his family."

I took the little pink piglet out of my pocket and handed it to Joan. When she saw it, she cried. She'd thought that it had been lost.

"He bought it for Amy when she was three. John used to buy toys for the kids every time he came home. Where did you find it?"

"John gave it to me. He...he died in my arms. I'm sorry, but I couldn't do anything to save him. I wasn't fast enough."

"How did it happen?"

At first I didn't want to talk about it. I thought that it would be better for her not to know all the details. Then I remembered how relieved my mum had felt when she heard that my father had saved someone else's life. She felt better, because she knew that he didn't die for nothing. Joan deserved the truth. She deserved to know everything.

"His last words were that he loved you. He wanted me to tell you this. He told us everything about you, how you met and ran away, because your father didn't want you to marry him. He loved you more than anything."

When I finished my story, Joan was devastated, but I saw a little smile on her face. I was sure that she was remembering all the crazy stuff they had done and how much they loved each other. Just as I had loved Daniela.

After I left John's house, I didn't go straight back to the station. I loved the smell of the sea and the sound of the waves crashing onto the beach. It was the middle of October. The sky was full of silver clouds that danced along with the wind. I felt safe, just as when I used to walk down the beach with Daniela. She would say that she hated the way her hair blew when we were on the beach. She thought that she looked as though she had a pigeon's nest on her head. I'd been so busy lately that I hadn't had time to think about her. I realised that I had forgotten many things from our relationship. Sometimes I couldn't even remember her voice.

As I walked down the beach, thinking about her, my phone rang. I didn't want to pick it up, because I wasn't in the mood to talk with anyone. Sergeant Griffiths's name was on the display, so I answered.

"Johnson, I heard that you were back."

"Yes, sir."

"Listen, I spoke with some of my colleagues at the RAF academy about you. They would like to know if you're interested in joining the air force."

"This is a great honour, sir, but I'm afraid that I had low grades on my GCSEs."

"I know that, Johnson. You'd have to sign up for a course and complete them again. They are willing to wait for you, because your performance in Afghanistan was outstanding. My colleagues think that you are a perfect match for their team."

"I will let you know in a few days, sir. Thank you for the offer. I appreciate it."

On my way back to London, I couldn't stop thinking about John and the nightmares I'd been having since he'd died in my arms. I would wake up in the middle of the night with sweat all over my body, just as my father did. I was happy that I had the opportunity to follow my father's path, but on the other hand, I wasn't sure if I could go back to the hell of the last two years.

I hadn't shown my friends how afraid I was every time we went on a mission or every night when I went to bed. I comforted most of them at night and cheered them up when they were down, but deep inside of me, I was afraid. Not just afraid—I was terrified. The things I'd seen: violence, death, hunger. I didn't want to go back there, but I knew that I didn't have a choice. And as scared as I was, I was honoured that I could do something meaningful with my life.

The only things that had kept me going through all the months I'd spent in the desert were Emma's letters. I thought about her often lately. She had this ability to make me feel good, protected, when I didn't have any hope. She made me laugh, when I wanted to cry. I had no idea that a person could do this just by sending a letter. She was special.

CHAPTER 19

After my trip to Southend-on-Sea, time passed very fast. I signed up for a three-month course so I could retake the GCSE exams. I always knew that I should've been a better student, but at the time I didn't really care. It was quite an experience to be back in college and to study as never before. I met a lot of friendly people there, but I wasn't interested in relationships, although I did go out with the group a few times. All I cared about was getting good grades so I could follow my father's path.

My mum was not very happy about my decision, but she wasn't surprised either. She knew how much I admired my dad. I stayed at Stephen's house until all the documents for the mortgage and the house came through. I didn't have enough money for the first instalment, so I borrowed some from Derek and some from my mum. He was more excited than she was. He was already planning big parties with naked women and disco balls on the ceiling. Oh, and let's not forget the dance floor. Since we'd got back from Afghanistan, he'd joined a salsa club, where he went every Saturday. I have to admit that he was a great dancer. He danced as well as he played basketball. Derek always knew how to make me laugh and how to change my mood. He really was my best friend, and I didn't mind him making plans for my house. I knew that he was joking, except for the parties.

Emma wanted to help me with the instalment as well, but I didn't let her. I would never borrow money or ask for help from a woman.

A few years back, it would've been a different story, but I had changed so much that even my mother hardly recognized me. I was glad that my life as a dealer was over. I'd never got caught, but I can't imagine what would've happened to me by now if I hadn't met Daniela. I would probably be in prison or worse—dead. I'd heard that Nigel had been killed in prison. My mum used to go insane because of me. The police would come to our place and ask questions about me and about my friends, but I was never around. I didn't keep any drugs where I lived. The police had no chance to catch me, but Nigel and his brother were stupid. They got arrested a few times. Kevin got shot, because he sold coke in someone else's territory. I couldn't imagine how stupid I had been to live like that. But in North London, you don't have a big choice: you either sell or take drugs, or you become a builder. The third option was to live on benefits for the rest of your life. There were people who had normal jobs that paid well, but they were lucky. The environment I'd lived in had dragged me down, until my angel saved me.

It had been difficult for Daniela to convince me to stop taking drugs. At first I stopped for a month or two, but when I went to a party, I couldn't help myself, especially if it was a house party. But when I saw Daniela's face, praying that I would stop, I felt guilty. She didn't mind when I was high, but she didn't like it either. Although when we went to Amsterdam, she smoked with me. Ever since then she hadn't wanted to eat fish. God knows why. She told me it was looking at her, and she was scared of it.

I missed her so much. She always knew what to say to make me feel better. And after all the mistakes I'd made, after all the people I'd hurt, she made me feel like a better a person. She made me forget my past.

I moved into my house in Windsor two months later. It was officially mine. Even though it had been very well maintained, it had a few cracks in the ceiling, and some of the rooms needed repainting. I hated the magnolia colour. But there it was, my house, just the way I remembered it.

I spent about a month making everything the way I wanted it. I painted the bedroom orange. I'd always wanted an orange bedroom. My mum would never let me do this in our old place, and to be honest, even if she had let me, I wouldn't have done it then, because I was too lazy. Emma helped me with the living room, because it was quite big. I will never forget that day we spent painting. She threw things at me every time I joked about her not doing it right.

Since I didn't have a kitchen yet, we had to eat at her place. She was a really good cook. I joked about her leaving Ealing Studios to become a chef at the Dorchester. I really enjoyed myself when I was with her. She was the only one who saw the house before the refurbishment. I didn't want to let anyone else in until I'd finished with everything. I didn't have much time, though, because of the courses. And I wanted to finish before I entered the academy. That's why I was grateful that Emma decided to help me, even though it was for two days over a weekend.

"It will be easier if you use the small brush for the edges."

"Oh, shut up. I'm doing it right."

"No, you think that you're doing it right, but you're not. Listen to me. I'm a professional."

"And how long did you work as a labourer exactly?"

"A few months."

"That doesn't make you an expert."

"Oh, yeah?" I took the smallest brush and dunked it in the paint. "Watch me now."

"What are you doing?"

"You'll see."

"Why are you coming so close? Move away with that brush, Ben..."

"You've missed one spot."

I came closer and grabbed her. Emma screamed, but I didn't let her go. Instead I pained her nose and one of her cheeks white. Once she freed herself, she took another brush and ran after me.

"You'll be sorry, Ben."

"But only if you catch me."

"I run the London marathon! I will catch you."

"And I'm a trained soldier. Good luck."

We chased each other for a while and then got back to what we were doing. She didn't get the chance to get back at me until the next day, when she attacked me from behind.

Emma said, "Since you're a trained soldier, how come you didn't see that coming?"

I grabbed her and held her so close to me that I could feel her heart beating. For the first time since Daniela's death, I felt goose bumps. I'd only wanted to paint her face white, but when I looked at her beautiful eyes, I stopped breathing. She looked at me the same way Daniela did, and for a moment I felt an urge to kiss her red lips. And there I was, standing in front of this beautiful woman, not knowing what to do. I thought that if I kissed her, I would be cheating on Daniela. I was sure that Emma wanted the same thing I did, but instead of giving in to the feelings I must have had for months now, I pushed her away and didn't say anything.

After that happened, I hid from Emma for a while, but she didn't call me either. I saw her once from my window and waved at her, instead of going out to talk with her as I had before. I didn't know what was going on with me. I'd decided to run away, just as I'd done before.

It took me about a month to finish with the refurbishment and another two weeks to get the garden ready. Even though it was wintertime, I wanted at least to clean up all the garbage from it and get it in shape for the spring. Once I was ready, I decided that the first people to see the place should be my mum and Stephen. I knew that it would be very difficult for her to come back here. All the memories, all the pain would come back to her.

Even though everything was different, when she entered the front door, she rushed to the bedroom she'd shared with my dad. After that she went straight to the back garden. All the flowers she'd taken care of when she'd lived here were gone, except for the daisies near the fence. The strange thing was that daisies usually don't grow during this time of the year, but these seemed as if they were waiting for her to see them. My mum went up to them, holding Lizzie by the hand. She knelt next to them, cut one off, and put it in Lizzie's hair. My little sister smiled and said that she looked like a princess. During dinner my mum didn't say a word. I realised that even though so many years had passed since she'd lost my father, she still loved him. She would never forget him. Unfortunately, I wasn't brave enough to move on with my life, as she had done.

For two weeks I'd been trying to avoid Emma. I went out very early in the morning to train, and I spent most of the rest of my time inside the house. I managed to unpack all my stuff from my mother's house and arrange it. There was no point, though, because I had to leave for Cranwell in three weeks. I couldn't wait, not only because I was about to make my dreams come true, but because I would have an excuse to leave Emma and my personal life behind for three years. Cranwell was 120 miles away from Windsor, which was far enough for me. I knew that I would end up being the strange loner, feeding the squirrels and pigeons just like Mrs Martin, but I didn't care.

I would run at the park every evening around six o'clock. I wanted to keep in shape, and I slept better if I was tired. Every time I passed by one of the benches near the river, I saw Mrs Martin, but I didn't want to stop and talk to her. I was scared that I would be doing the same thing as her someday. But the day before Derek and Karisha visited me, I saw the old lady with tears in her eyes. I just couldn't pass by her again, so I stopped.

"Mrs Martin, I'm Ben Johnson. Do you remember me?"

She raised her head and looked at me with her bright blue eyes. The years hadn't spared her. Her face was full of wrinkles, but she still looked pretty. When she smiled at me, I felt guilty for passing by her. This woman, as much as she had suffered in her life, had a generous heart.

"Of course I remember you, dear. You are Patrick's son. He was a great man, may God bless his soul. How are you, dear?"

"I'm OK, Mrs Martin."

"Oh, please, honey, call me Cici. I know that I'm old, but my heart is still young. Not according to the doctors, but who listens to what they say?"

I laughed. "Well, we should listen to them sometimes."

"At my age, it doesn't matter, dear."

"Don't talk like that! You still have many years left."

"Maybe, but I have to spend them all alone. I don't have anyone left—no husband, no children, no grandchildren. My life is empty."

"Is that the reason you come here every day?"

"Yes. I used to feed the pigeons with my husband. That's how we met. But he's gone. I don't even remember his voice anymore. Most of my memories are gone. I'm old, and I tend to forget so many things. I have only a few photos of him. Today is the anniversary of his death—sixty-seven years ago."

"I'm sorry, Mrs Martin. I wish I could do something for you."

"I've seen you with that pretty girl, Emma. She is a nice woman, always polite with me."

"Yes, I know. She's a good friend of mine."

Mrs Martin took my hand and patted it. "Don't run away from happiness, dear."

"I don't know what you're talking about."

"I've seen the way she looks at you. And I'm sure that you feel the same way, but for some reason, you are running away from it."

"That's not true."

"As you say, dear. When my husband died, I spent years in pain, because he was the only man I'd ever loved. Five or six years later, I met a man who fell madly in love with me. Don't look at me like that, boy. I was young and pretty once. He asked me to marry him, but I refused. I didn't want to move on, and that was a mistake. I regret that I left my chance for happiness behind. The man got married, and he has seven grandchildren. Think about it."

"I...I will."

It was nice talking to you, dear."

"Mrs Martin, would you like to come over for a cup of tea tomorrow?"

"I'd love to. But only if you invite the lovely young lady to join us."

Mrs Martin stood up and headed back to her house, while I thought about our conversation. She was right. I knew that she was right. The only problem was that I was afraid. What if I lost Emma, too? What if it didn't work? How was I supposed to keep up a long-distance relationship? I wasn't ready for this. I wasn't able to give Emma what she truly deserved.

After I returned from jogging, I took a shower. The conversation with Mrs Martin came back to me. I couldn't explain it, but somehow the old woman knew what was going on with me. I felt that I had to see Emma and talk to her, so I put my jacket on and knocked on her door. It was nine o'clock, and she opened the door wearing a dressing gown. She looked surprised to see me, especially at this time of the evening.

"Ben, what a surprise! Come in. Is there something wrong?"

"No, I just wanted to see you."

I sat on the sofa in the living room. She came back from the kitchen with two glasses of wine. She'd been watching *CSI Miami*. I'd watched it a long time ago, but I preferred *Las Vegas*. Emma and I talked for hours. I apologised for my behaviour during the past few weeks, but I didn't tell her what the real reason was. I was afraid to share my story about Daniela with anyone, because I wanted to keep her only for myself.

At about one o'clock I decided that I ought to leave. I hadn't even realised how late it was until I looked at my watch. Emma came with me to the door, and we stayed there for another five minutes. I didn't know if it was the wine or Mrs Martin's voice in my head, but suddenly I felt the urge to hold her in my arms. I drew close to her and kissed her. She put her soft hand on my cheek, and I smelled the scent of strawberries. I didn't want to stop. For a moment I felt as if I never wanted to leave this woman. If I spent another minute without her, I would die.

She took my hand and pulled me back inside the house. I followed her to the bedroom. I slowly took her dressing gown off as she was helping me out of my T-shirt. I was shaking, because she was the first woman I'd had feelings for since Daniela. But at that moment, Daniela wasn't there. She was out of my thoughts. The scent of Emma's skin and the touch of her soft lips made me forget about the only woman I'd ever loved.

When I woke up the next morning, Emma wasn't in the bed. I smelled freshly frying bacon and eggs. I put on my clothes. When I went downstairs, I saw her holding a frying pan. I was speechless. She looked amazing, even though her hair was tied in a ponytail and she wasn't wearing any makeup. She was so beautiful that anyone would have fallen in love with her. I knew that I was already in love with her. We sat at the table and ate breakfast, just as I used to do with Daniela. All the memories of her came back with the morning coffee. I felt as if I'd betrayed her, but it was too late. I was falling in love with Emma, and no matter how much guilt I carried inside of me, I knew that I wouldn't be able to leave Emma. Not now, when I felt happy for the first time since I'd lost Daniela.

Derek came with Karisha for a few days. I was surprised to find out that the two of them were dating. It turned out that he'd somehow found her on Facebook and invited her on a date. She thought that he was completely crazy, but eventually went out with him. I'd never seen Karisha with a man. I knew that she was a romantic girl, and I was happy that she'd found Derek, because he would make any woman happy. He knew how to treat them, and no matter what people said about him, he wasn't a womanizer. They were surprised to find out that Emma and I were together. I was afraid of what Karisha would say, but she was happy. She told me that I deserved to move on and find love again. And for the first time, I agreed with her.

CHAPTER 20

Three weeks passed. It was time for me to leave Windsor and spend thirty-six weeks at Cranwell. My only concern was that I wouldn't be able to see Emma very often. Even though I was able to go back to Windsor every two weeks, it wouldn't be the same. Besides, we had just started our relationship. We were in the honeymoon phase, where everything was perfect. We spent hours in the park, shared romantic dinners, and watched movies all night. Mrs Martin came every afternoon for a cup of tea. I have to say that her face had completely changed after a few weeks with us. She didn't feel so lonely. Since Emma's parents lived in another city, she would have someone to talk to, and she wouldn't be too lonely.

I had no idea what I should expect once I got there. I'd read everything on their website, and Sergeant Griffiths had explained it all to me. I was still afraid, in a way, maybe because I was finally going to make my dream come true. It was something that I'd always wanted. There were times when I'd thought that it would never happen. I thought that I wasn't good enough. And now that I had the chance to try, I wanted to give it my best, to be the first in the course, to make my father proud. I really wished that he were there to give me support and advice. It would've been easier for me if he were around.

Before I left for Cranwell, I decided to visit his grave. I managed to clean up the ivy from the tombstone and pull all the skunk. I took care of his last resting place, just as he used to take care of me when I was a little boy. I brought Emma with me, because I didn't want to be alone. Since I'd never got the chance to introduce him to Daniela, I thought that it would be the right thing to do. He would've been happy for me. He'd liked Emma when we were kids. She was always jumping around him, asking questions about the other soldiers, admiring him for his courage. Sometimes I felt that he liked her more than he liked me.

Emma helped me with the luggage, not that I had that much to carry with me. I had many concerns about the house, but she promised that she would take care of it. I knew that it hadn't been the right time to buy a house. I didn't have much money left because of that, but I hadn't wanted to lose the house again. I was going to be paid during my officer training, and I hoped that it would be enough to pay my mortgage every month.

Once my bags were ready, I sat on the sofa in the living room to relax. Emma sat next to me, and I hugged her. It was about eight o'clock in the evening and I was getting hungry. Derek had said that he would pick me up in his car at 6:00 a.m. I'd decided to go to bed early that night.

"Emma, I'm hungry. I'll order pizza. Do you want one as well?"

"Actually I have a better idea. Why don't you come over to my house and have dinner with me? I think I have a chicken in the fridge."

"I'm tired and really hungry. I don't think that I could wait until you cooked that chicken."

"Oh, come on! Do this for me, please!"

"OK, OK! I just can't say no to you."

When we entered the dining room, I saw two candles on the table, along with plates and cutlery. Emma had set the table for dinner. I could smell the chicken in the oven. For a moment I stayed at the door, watching her take out a tray from the cooker. I thought how lucky I was to have her. I was probably the happiest man on earth, because I'd been able to find love again. Emma eased the pain of Daniela's death. She was still in my heart, but not during that night. That night was all about Emma. I gave her my full attention, because I knew that she needed it. I wondered why she'd chosen me. I still couldn't figure out why Daniela chose me, either. Both of them were beautiful, and many men were attracted to them. Emma was a treasure, and I had no intention of losing her.

After we finished with dinner, she invited me upstairs. I saw candles everywhere. There were rose petals, and I smelled the scent of lavender in the air. This reminded me of the night I'd planned to propose to Daniela. I didn't want to think about that at the moment. It was something that I should've forgotten a long time ago, but I hadn't, and now wasn't the time to think about it. Emma unbuttoned my shirt and kissed me. I was nervous, and I think that she noticed. It wasn't because I was leaving the next morning; it was because while we made love, for the first time I was thinking about Daniela, not Emma. At that moment, I realised how much I missed her. It wasn't fair to Emma, but Daniela was still part of my life, even though she was gone.

"What are you thinking about?"

"Nothing. I'm just tired."

"Are you sure?"

"Yes, I'm fine."

"Ben, can I ask you something?"

"Yes, go on."

"Who's Daniela?"

My pupils dilated. I turned and sat on the bed. I didn't know what to say. I didn't know what answer to give. How did she find out about Daniela? Karisha must have told her. I'd asked her not to talk about Daniela and me to other people. How was I going to explain to Emma who Daniela was? I wasn't ready for this. I wasn't ready to talk about her yet.

"Ben? Who's Daniela?"

"Who told you about her?"

"I found a letter addressed to her and..."

"Why are you reading my letters? Who gave you permission?" I was frustrated. I didn't think that Emma would search my room and read my letters.

"I didn't read it. I just saw her name on it. I found it in your drawer with a ring while I was looking for your shirts."

"You shouldn't touch my things!"

"Ben, stop shouting. I'm sorry if I offended you. I just want to know. I think that I have the right to know. Are you having an affair? Or is the affair with me?"

"What are you talking about? I'm not having an affair with anyone."

"Then who is she? Why do you have a picture of her in your wallet? Because that's her, isn't it?"

"Emma, I don't want to talk about it."

"I have the right to know!"

"You have no right to know anything. This is my life, not yours. I don't want to talk about it. End of conversation."

I got dressed and ran back to my house. I shouldn't have shouted at her, and I was sure that she must have cried after I left. I didn't have the courage to tell her my story. I wasn't ready yet. When she mentioned Daniela's name, I was shocked. Daniela once was everything I'd wanted from this life, and I still couldn't accept the fact that she was gone. I felt that if I talked about her and the accident, she would be gone forever. I knew that I should've left her behind and continued my life with Emma or another woman. I knew that I should've asked Emma for a picture and left Daniela's somewhere no one could find it. I knew that she should've stayed just a memory from my past, but for me she was still alive. And as much as I loved Emma, I loved Daniela more, and I didn't know if that was ever going to change.

I woke up early the next morning. I was feeling guilty for the way I'd treated Emma, so I decided that it would be best if I apologised to her. When I went out in the garden, I assumed that she was still asleep, so I wrote her a letter and put through the mail slot on the door, along with the spare keys for my house. It wasn't the best way to apologise, and I had no idea if she would ever forgive me, but I hoped for the best.

Four weeks passed. I didn't have any news from Emma. I wondered if she would ever talk to me again. I was afraid to go back to Windsor and see her. I had no idea what I was going to tell her. At least I had plenty of things to do at Cranwell. During those four weeks I had to learn the basic military skills. Even though I'd been through this training already, I didn't mind having something to do while I waited for Emma's phone call or letter. Besides, I managed to improve my shooting skills. Derek joined the RAF along with me. He said that no matter what happened, he would always be with me wherever I went. He thought that we were some kind of separated Siamese twins.

Derek went to London every two weeks to see Karisha. Those two were making my life crazy. They would talk until midnight or one o'clock, and since Derek was my roommate, I wasn't able to sleep. I was happy for them though. They made a great couple, unlike Emma and me.

The next five weeks we spent learning different techniques and having fun with the leadership exercises, in which Derek always wanted to be the boss. The first term passed, and there was still no call or letter from Emma. I became desperate. I wanted to call her and hear her voice, but I wasn't sure she would pick up the phone. Derek threw my phone at me a few times, but he realised there was no way to make me call her, so he gave up.

I thought that there was no hope for Emma and me to be together again, until one day, after twenty-two weeks, she called me. I couldn't believe my eyes when I saw her name on the display of my phone.

"Hello?"

"Hi, Ben."

"Hey...How are you."

"I'm fine, thanks. And how are you doing?"

"Not bad. I've been very busy lately with all the courses. Look, Emma, I'm so sorry for that night."

"Ben, I'm calling you to let you know that there's been a leakage in the kitchen, and I called a plumber. He changed one of the pipes."

"Oh, ok. I'll give you the money once I get back to Windsor."

"Don't worry about it. I have to go now. Take care."

"Wait, Emma! Did you read the letter?"

"I have to go, Ben. Let me know when you're home so I can give you back the key. Take care."

"Thanks! You too."

That phone call made me realise that I had made another stupid mistake in my life. I can't even remember how many people I have hurt. I couldn't stop thinking about Emma, and I knew that I had to go back to Windsor as soon as possible. I couldn't even enjoy my first flight with a plane. Even though I wasn't alone while I flew, I felt free. I could feel the adrenaline in my heart, the blood pumping in my veins. It was incredible! And yet I was thinking about Emma. The strange thing was that I'd wanted to become a pilot, not only because of my father, but because I believed that I would be closer to Daniela. But now I could only think of Emma and how to get her back.

When I arrived at Windsor Station, I was shaking. I couldn't feel my feet or hands. I was barely able to hold my sack. I had never been that nervous before in my life, may be because it was the first time that I was about to apologise to someone I cared about, except my mum.

After leaving my sack at the house, I went straight to Emma's and knocked on her door. It was about 8 o'clock and I knew that she wasn't expecting me. I hoped that she would let me in so I could explain everything to her.

"Ben?"

"Hi, Emma. I'm sorry that I didn't call to let you know I was coming."

"It's OK. I'll go and get the keys."

"No, wait." I took her hand and felt her soft skin on my palm. I could again smell the scent of strawberries. "I really need to talk to you."

"I think that you said enough the other night."

"Let me just explain everything to you, please."

She looked at me, and I saw the sparkle in her beautiful blue eyes. She had no choice but to let me in; I was desperate and she knew it. Emma was a proud woman, and I knew that even if she heard everything I had to say, even if she accepted my apologies, it would be very difficult to win back her trust, to make her fall in love with me again.

I told her the whole story of my life. Everything, including the drugs, how I had met Daniela, and how I fell in love with her. I told her every detail of our life together, from the good moments to the fights we'd had.

When I got to the part about the marriage proposal, I stopped. I didn't know if I had the courage to go back to that night. Emma took my hand in hers and caressed my cheek. Her touch gave me strength, and I finished my story.

"It wasn't easy to move on with my life, Emma. You're the first person I've talked to about this. When Daniela died, my mum asked me if I wanted to talk to a specialist, and I got so upset that I didn't speak to her for a month. Even Derek doesn't know anything about her. He's asked me a few times about the tattoo on my back, but I've never told him. Emma, I'm really sorry if I have offended you in any way. You're the best thing that has happened to me since I lost Daniela. I thought that I would never be able to be with another woman, but then I met you. Please forgive me."

For a few minutes, Emma stood opposite me as I sat on the sofa. She was speechless. My heart was jumping so fast that even she could hear it beating. I waited patiently for her to answer, without saying a word. All of a sudden, she drew close to me and kissed me. Then she took my hand and led me to her bedroom.

We made love until the morning. It was the best night of my life. I hugged Emma and kissed her left shoulder. She turned, and when I saw her face, I knew that something bad was coming.

"Ben, listen. I had a great time last night, but it was for the last time."

"What are you talking about? I don't understand."

"I can't be with you, because you still love her. She's still part of your life and I can't compete with an angel, because that's how you think of her, isn't it? She will always be part of your life, part of our relationship. I can't live with this."

"Emma, that's not true."

"Isn't it? Thean tell me, Ben, do you love me?"

I knew that I should say, "Yes, yes, I love you more than anything in my life," but I couldn't. I couldn't say it, so I just stood there, next to her, thinking how much more I could actually ruin things between us.

"So I thought. Go back to Afghanistan, Ben, and when you come back, call me, but only if you can say those three words to me. Otherwise, forget about me. It would be better if we didn't see each other again."

CHAPTER 21

I couldn't feel my legs. There wasn't enough air in the plane. I was falling, and I knew that I was going to die. There was no hope for me, not anymore. I couldn't eject myself from the plane, and I didn't know what to do, except to close my eyes and wait for death to come for me. I didn't even know where the shot had come from. I didn't see anyone on the ground or in the sky. I couldn't believe that on my first mission as a pilot, I would fail.

All I could think of now was Emma. Her last words to me were, "What if I'm your only chance for happiness? You haven't realised it yet, but you will one day. I hope that it's not too late, though."

I'd spent five months in Afghanistan, and she hadn't sent me a single letter. I wondered if she'd found someone else and if she was happy. I'd never told her that I loved her, that I cared about her and wanted to be with her for the rest of my life, because I was too busy thinking about my past, about my problems, and I thought that she would never understand.

I never said good-bye to her, or to my mum, my little sis, or Karisha. What was going to happen with my body? Would they find it among the burning parts of the aeroplane? Would Emma cry for me? I was only twenty-four years old. I hadn't done anything significant with my life. I'd hurt so many people, and I wondered what God would have to say about it.

All I could see behind me were the golden sands of the desert. I felt the heat coming from one of the wings. I was falling like a hawk with a broken wing. I knew that Derek was behind me somewhere, but he couldn't do anything to save me. He was my best friend, and I'd never told him that he was like the brother I'd never had. I heard one of the officers on the radio, asking if I could eject, but I was too weak to answer. I felt the blood coming from my shoulder and wondered if my father had had the same thoughts I did at this moment.

I closed my eyes and imagined that I was back in London, sitting on a bench in the park, smelling the grass. I would complain about the noise every time the gardener cut it, but I enjoyed the freshness in the air when I opened the window afterwards. I'd had so many dreams: I wanted to start a family, become a lecturer, but none of that would happen. I had no future, no dreams, and no hope for survival. The one thing I prayed for wasn't my life, but forgiveness.

My time was coming, I could feel it. I wondered if there would be a light, just as everyone said. I kept my eyes closed until the end, until I heard a sound that reminded me of thunder. I was alone in the desert. I managed to get out of the plane somehow, but I couldn't feel my legs. The pain in my right shoulder was gone, but there was still blood coming out of it. The last thing I saw before losing conscious was the picture of Daniela, burning. I tried to reach it, but I was too weak to move.

✈

I woke up at Bruce Castle Park, by the old oak tree where I had picnics with Daniela. It was sunny, and I smelled the fresh grass. I couldn't believe that there was no one around. It was quiet, and I was able to hear my heartbeat. I didn't know how I'd got there or who had brought me, and then I saw her. There was a woman coming towards me in a white dress. Her hair was brown, and the wind was waving her curls around. I knew who this woman was, but I couldn't believe my eyes. After all these years, I was finally seeing her again, Daniela. She approached me and smiled. Her teeth were as white as pearls. I stood up and watched her. I wanted to remember this moment forever.

"You're here! I can't believe my eyes! You're here."
"Ben, you should go home."
"No, I want to stay here with you. I can't live without you."
"I'm not real, Ben. You should go home."
"I don't want to go home, Daniela!"
"You must let me go, Ben."
"How can I do that? How can I live without you?"
"It's time to go, Ben. Just let me go."

She turned away, and I tried to follow her, but I couldn't move. I shouted after her and felt the warmth of the tears on my cheek.

"Daniela! Daniela! Come back!"
"Ben, please let me go. Just let me go."
"I want to be with you! Please don't leave me again! Don't leave me alone!"
"You are not alone. You will never be, Ben."
"I love you."

When I opened my eyes, the first person I saw was Derek. He was standing next to my bed. I didn't know where I was or what was going on. I remember that I was moving and there were a lot of people around me. My sight was blurry, and there were people talking about blood loss and an operation. One thing was sure, I wasn't dead. I'd survived the crash somehow. Some would say that I was a lucky man to cheat death twice. But I thought that I hadn't deserved a second chance, and definitely not a third one.

"Hey, bro! You're awake. How do you feel?"
"I can't feel my legs."
"It's OK, you are still weak."
"Where am I?"

"You're back in London, bro. I saved your white ass from the ashes of your plane. You know, for someone who brags about what a great pilot he is, you suck, man."

"Derek, that's not funny."

"I'm sorry. How do you feel?"

"Like a smashed cockroach."

"Who's having fun now? Your mum went home. You were in a coma for two weeks. They moved you from base hospital a few days ago. Shall I call her?"

"No, wait. Where's Emma?"

"She's outside. Do you want to see her?"

"Yes!"

"Yes, yes...give orders to the black man. Don't thank him for saving your life. And you are supposed to be my best buddy."

"Derek, seriously man! Stop making fun of me, and call Emma. Thank you for saving my life! Happy?"

"Very!"

When the door opened, my heart jumped. I'd never thought that I would see her again, but I wasn't prepared for what came next. Emma came into the room, and I saw her beautiful smile. She wore a yellow dress and her blonde hair was tied in a bun. She looked so beautiful that my breath stopped for a moment.

I was so busy looking at her gentle face that I didn't notice her baby bump until she came closer to me. She saw the look on my face and smiled.

"The doctor says that it's a boy."

"What? When?"

"Ben, relax! Don't push yourself too much. You just woke up."

"No, I want to know! Why didn't you tell me?"

"I didn't want you to feel obliged."

"Obliged? Emma, this is what I always wanted."

"How do you feel?"

"My whole body hurts, but I'm the luckiest, and happiest, man on earth. "

"I think that I should go now. The doctors will come very soon to check if you are OK."

"Emma?"

"Yes?"

"I love you!"

She sat on the bed and kissed me. Even though my whole body was in pain, I smiled. I was finally going to be happy and have my own family. Daniela was right. I wasn't alone and was never going to be.

THE END